Third Time's the Charm

Robyn C Rye

Published by robyncrye, 2020.

Also by Robyn C Rye

Farnsworth Sisters
Marrying a Rogue
Rescuing Hannah

The Buckingham Sisters
Lady Maggie's Challenge
Layla's Unwanted Husband

The Evans Family
Sometimes Love is not Enough
Still the One
Moving Forward

Standalone
One More Chance
Lady Jayne's Reputation
Third Time's the Charm
Can't Stop Loving You

The Marriage Scam
An Unlikely Match
Searching For You
The Unexpected Suitor
The Lady and the Duke
Starting Over
An Unforgettable Stranger
The Duke's Revenge
The Temporary Wife
Against The Odds
Betrayed
No Good Turn Goes Unpunished
Lady Eloise's Soldier
Lillian's Forbidden Beau
Remember Me
Always Second Best
When One Door Closes
Coming Home to You
Chasing Shadows
Fool Me Once
Deserting Lady Audrey
My Unlikely Saviour
Lies and Deception
A New Beginning
Julia's Second Chance
The Hidden Enemy
The Maiden's Redemption
Miss Elizabeth's Season

Table of Contents

Author's note...1
Chapter One..2
Chapter Two..8
Chapter Three..12
Chapter Four...18
Chapter Five...22
Chapter Six..25
Chapter Seven..28
Chapter Eight..33
Chapter Nine...40
Chapter Ten..43
Chapter Eleven...48
Chapter Twelve...54
Chapter Thirteen...58
Chapter Fourteen...65
Chapter Fifteen..69
Chapter Sixteen..74
Chapter Seventeen..79
Chapter Eighteen...84
Chapter Nineteen...89
Chapter Twenty...93
Chapter Twenty-One...99
Chapter Twenty-Two..102
Chapter Twenty-Three..106
Chapter Twenty-Four...112
Chapter Twenty-Five...117
Chapter Twenty-Six..122
Epilogue..127

Author's note

Thank you for joining me in telling the story of Jo Bromley. I hope you enjoyed her story as much as I did recounting it. If you liked the book and have a minute, I would appreciate a brief review on the page or site where you purchased it. Reviews from readers like you make a significant difference in helping new readers discover stories like Third Time's the Charm. Your help in spreading the word is greatly appreciated.

Thank you!

Robyn C Rye

. . . .

Robyncrye.author@gmail.com

Loud music drowned out conversation, although few people were interested in chatting. The beat of the music thumped through Jo's brain, and she gritted her teeth against the vibration. Lights flashed on and off. The dance floor was filled with groups of girls dressed in skimpy clothes. Occasionally, a couple danced into view, but they weren't dancing as much as they made out to be on the dance floor. *What the hell am I doing here?* she wondered. Once again, her workmates had played her for a sucker. The girls at work had a girls' night out, and as Jo wasn't a big drinker, she had offered to act as the designated driver.

The night had started well, with the group seated together at tables, chatting, laughing, and drinking. For the first time in her working life, she felt like a member of this exclusive group. After their first few drinks, her bubble burst when the girls wandered off, searching for male companions. Jo watched in despair as girl after girl hooked up with a male partner. The girls in her group, who hadn't found a partner, moved onto the dance floor to dance together.

Jo's head was pounding. The club was hot, and she could feel perspiration trickle down her back and pool under her arms. The excess weight she carried meant that she always felt warm, and in this room crowded with feverish bodies and inadequate air conditioning, it felt like a sauna. She had dressed in a conservative outfit tonight, but nothing looked good on her at one hundred and twenty kilos. She cursed herself for being a fool, realising she shouldn't have come. Now, it was apparent that these women were not real friends, and they had used her as their taxi home, whenever that might be. Did she have to keep up her part of the bargain, considering the friends who were supposed to hang out together had not upheld their end of the deal?

As she looked around, trying to make eye contact with one woman from work, Jo noticed a group of men huddled at a table halfway across the room. Now and then, a man would look over his shoulder and snigger. Gales of laughter followed, and Jo had a good idea of what would come. Her thought proved correct when a man rose and walked towards her. He was an impressive specimen of a man. His designer jeans hugged him tightly, and his crew-neck shirt moulded muscles that had probably taken hours at the gym to perfect. Sandy brown hair, styled to display his abundant locks best, topped off a perfect face, all chiselled cheeks and square jaw. This man was way out of Jo's league, and his approach must have been because one of his friends dared him to chat her up. She had been the butt of cruel jokes before; she recognised that her excessive weight was always why men thought she was fair game.

"May I sit here?" he asked politely.

Jo scrutinised him. "This is obviously of enormous amusement to your friends. Please don't insult my intelligence by pretending to be interested in me. Tell your mates you asked me for a date or whatever their dare was, and leave me in peace."

The man pressed his hand dramatically against his heart.

"You wound me! I would never be so callous as to make you the butt of a joke. I wanted to chat with you to see why you are sitting alone and not dancing with your friends."

"I was stupid enough to offer to act as the designated driver, and the others aren't friends, more work colleagues."

"I should introduce myself. I'm Chase Donaldson, and I work as a sales agent at a BMW dealer in the city."

"My name is Josephine Bromley, and I work in town as a manager at a PR firm."

"There, that wasn't too hard, was it?"

"Chase, you appear to be a good man. Why don't you chat up one of the other girls more susceptible to your charms? Surely you must have won your bet by now?!"

"Josephine, you are such a doubter. I am not in the middle of a wager and have no dubious motives. Why don't we chat and see where it goes?"

Jo looked beyond Chase's shoulder; his mates were still glancing over their shoulders and sniggering.

"Have a look at your buddies. Their sniggers and covert looks suggest you have a mean prank in mind for me. Your motives aren't without purpose."

While she had been talking with Chase, her workmates had noticed the exchange and drifted over. Suzanne, a blond, tall, and voluptuous woman, sidled up to Chase. "Hi, honey. Jo is a bit uptight, but I could give you a good time. Do you want to dance with me?"

Jo knew how this would go; Chase would thank her for the chat and disappear with Suzanne for the rest of the night.

Chase raked his gaze over Suzanne's breasts and down her waist, paused at her crotch, and slid down her legs. He said, "Thanks for the offer, but we are okay here." Jo nearly passed out in surprise. Suzanne's open mouth and wide eyes attested to her feelings at being turned down. She stomped around and then stalked away from the table. Chase laughed out loud.

"I don't think she gets many knockbacks. It'll do her good."

Jo shook her head in amazement.

"You just turned down Suzanne to sit and talk to me. Are you gay?"

His loud barking laugh startled her.

"You don't pull any punches, do you? No, I am not gay, but I don't need sloppy seconds from some woman who's had her back against a wall out the back and her dress up around her waist."

"If you didn't come to hook up, why did you come here tonight?"

"Well, my friends decided we've worked hard all week and needed a break. Speaking of my friends, I should go back and join them. I've enjoyed talking to you. Can I call you?"

His question bewildered Jo. "If you walk back to your friends and they all burst out laughing, I will dump the contents of my water jug on you. Do you understand?"

Chase grinned at her, and butterflies took flight in her stomach; a flush spread up her neck and over her face. She ducked her head. Chase placed a finger under her chin and lifted her face.

"That blush is cute; don't hide it from me. Now, Josephine, hand me your phone so I can put my number in it and here's my phone; please put your name in the contacts list."

Once Chase had the number, he handed her the phone and returned to sit with his friends. Jo looked over once or twice, and the mates weren't laughing. She caught Chase's eye at one stage, and he winked at her, sending the blush straight back up her neck to cover her face.

Eventually, her workmates called it a night, and the group departed. Suzanne, who was more than a little inebriated, sneered at her in the car.

"Think you're smart snagging a hottie tonight? He may have wanted to chat this evening, but he is way out of your league. You'd best forget him; guys like that don't go out with fat chicks like you."

Jo knew this was correct, but she wanted to believe it was real for once.

When the phone rang early the next day, Jo considered leaving it to voicemail. She was already running late for work; she didn't have time to talk to random marketers or charities begging for funds. With the shrill ring of her phone again, she double-backed and answered the call.

"Hello."

"Josephine? It's Chase here. Can you talk?"

"Ah, good morning, Chase. I'm running late, so I have little time to talk. Why don't you ring me back in an hour?"

"No need to ring back; meet me at Stratford's for coffee at five-thirty?"

Jo laughed. "Sure, see you then."

As she drove to work, Jo was happy. This sexy, agreeable man had just asked her to meet him for coffee. She tried to concentrate on her new customer information at work, but found that Chase's handsome face kept intruding. What if this was a joke? He had asked her to meet him, but would he show up? What if she arrived and he didn't show up? Doubts swirled through her head as her work required less time and concentration. Jo came up with a solution to her problem. She didn't want to sit at the cafe for hours waiting for a no-show. She could ask him if he was at the coffee shop if she arrived late. That way, she wouldn't need to put up with pitying looks from the servers when he left her stranded.

Before leaving work, Jo ran to the restroom to check her appearance. She headed for the car park with her hair smoothed down and a layer of gloss on her lips. The traffic, as always, was bumper to bumper until she cleared the main thoroughfare and drove along the side streets that led to the cafe. Once she parked, excitement and dread consumed Jo. Would Chase arrive, or would he stand her up?

With nerves racing, she stood outside the cafe to look through the window. Chase was not in the room. She backed away, waiting for five minutes before calling him. As she stood under the porch of a shop across the street, she saw Chase and an attractive blonde walk towards the café's door. The woman reached up and kissed Chase. He pulled her in close and closed his hand over her butt. She laughed and pushed his hand away, and then they parted; he went into the café, and she walked further along the street to the shops.

After witnessing the kiss between Chase and his girlfriend, Jo did not intend to participate in their scam. She dialled her phone and watched as Chase answered his phone through the window.

"Josephine, where are you? I'm waiting for you at the café."

"Sorry, Chase, something has come up. I'll have to cancel."

"Great, I cleared my calendar so we could get together, and now I'm at a loose end."

"I'm sure you'll catch up with your girlfriend if you hurry. After that passionate kiss, I'm sure she's ready for more."

Chase's response was a string of profanities, and the phone went dead.

Jo headed towards her car, feeling like a fool. Why had she believed Chase would pay attention to her? He had a girlfriend, a model, thin and attractive. Jo was glad she hadn't shared the excitement of meeting Chase with anyone else; at least she didn't need the false sympathy that would have flowed her way.

Burdened with fast food bags, Jo made her way home. There was no point in hanging around downtown now that she had cancelled the coffee date. Food had always been her consolation. As a child, she was shy around strangers, so she gravitated to the food tables at parties and functions. How much socialising could you do with your mouth full? The habit stuck, and while the shyness disappeared, the comfort eating remained entrenched.

Curled on her couch, she crammed food into her mouth as her mind focused on the latest reality TV show. People either loved or loathed reality shows; Jo loved them. The shows allow you to live vicariously through others when you have no life. She wished she were game enough to audition for a show, but knew her self-consciousness in public would prevent her from being chosen. The performances were for ratings, and reserved, fat people didn't appeal to an audience.

Lying in bed that night, Jo felt desolate. Her sobs had caused her a headache. When she got out of bed to find painkillers, the bathroom mirror revealed a woman with blotchy skin, red eyes, and rolls of loose fat. Self-pity was not an emotion that Jo allowed herself to experience often, but tonight, after Chase's dishonesty, she thought she deserved to indulge in it.

Chapter Two

The following day, Jo dragged herself to work. Her depression of the day before lingered, and she was abrupt with her workmates. Shortly after her morning tea break, the office lady came into her cubicle carrying an enormous bouquet.

"These are for you," she said with disapproval. "I don't think it's professional to have men sending flowers to a work environment."

Jo laughed. "How do you know they are from a man? I have been here for over five years and have never received a parcel at work. I'm certain you can overlook this one-time gift."

Extending her hand, Jo reached for the bouquet. She had a niggling idea of who it was from, but had no intention of opening the sealed envelope until the nosy woman left. Seated in her chair, she stared at the secretary. With a huff, the woman glared and then turned and left.

Jo pulled the envelope apart and read the folded note with trembling fingers.

'Josephine, I'm sorry about yesterday. I know the kiss looked bad, but Kelly and I are long-time friends, and she took me by surprise. My unfortunate response was automatic. Please give me another chance to get to know you. Chase.'

Jo left the phone call she needed to make until after work, not wanting to seem too eager. The flowers were a gracious gesture, but could she trust him? Nothing would change if she gave him another chance to get to know her; if it didn't work, she would still be alone. They agreed to meet at a different venue. Jo hurried towards the alternative meeting place; her heartbeat thudded at the same pace as her feet. Chase's apology sounded genuine, and she anticipated the meeting with hope. Jo scanned the room when she walked through the door, looking for Chase. As she approached the table, he stood, and her heart raced. He leaned forward to kiss her cheek. His gesture surprised Jo, but she looked composed, apart from a flush on her face.

"The other day was a mistake. Kelly tried to tease me, and her tactic worked, but we've known each other too long for it to go anywhere. Can you forgive me?"

"When I saw you in a passionate embrace right outside the coffee shop where we were to meet, I was angry with myself for thinking you liked me."

"I like you and want to get to know you. You have an inquiring mind and pull no punches; that's refreshing to a bloke like me."

"What type of bloke are you?"

"The kind that wears nice suits, drives a nice car, and looks okay. Girls only notice those things, and they believe I can fulfil their dream of a wealthy husband and a big house. Despite what others think, I'm not rich and don't enjoy women constantly trying to chat me up. Your friend the other night gave me the come-on that I always get. Is it wrong to want to be on good terms with someone before it goes further?"

Jo shook her head. How did you doubt a guy who appeared so apologetic? His version of events might be the truth, as she had never had a sexual response to anyone, so what would she know?

"I guess getting to know someone is the right way to start. If you're willing, we could spend time together."

"This is all new for me, Chase. I won't play games because I don't know how to be flirtatious. You will think I'm naïve, but I have done little socialising with men."

The smile he flashed her warmed her blood and made her heart pound. As they sipped their coffee, they chatted about public events and shared interests. Jo found Chase an excellent conversationalist, and the time together flew by. Chase suggested they meet for lunch in a few days, and she agreed. She felt overjoyed. This man might be Mr Right, and even if he wasn't, she intended to enjoy whatever time they had together.

The best time of Jo's life occurred over the following months. Chase wined and dined her in an old-fashioned way, and she wore a glow of happiness for all to see. The couple visited secluded restaurants and local tourist attractions she had never explored. The joy dimmed a little when she wondered why Chase never took her to restaurants and bars in the city. They had never met someone they knew on a date, and Jo wondered if Chase had deliberately chosen these places so that no one would see him in public with her. Sometimes, she would catch Chase following other women with his eyes and agonise over the meaning. Did all men, while out with their girlfriends, watch other women? Was this a man thing, or should his roving eye worry her? Jo wished she had a handbook on relationships; she was a novice and worried about making mistakes.

Chase and Jo spent three or four days a week together, but his busy work schedule sometimes interrupted their nights, and he would apologise and leave her to finish her meal alone. She could understand night call-outs if he were a doctor, but she doubted his excuses were valid as a car dealer. Who bought a car at night when the dealership closed at five o'clock? It crossed her mind to follow him one night and see where he went. Was he meeting his mates or another woman? Whatever the reason, his abandonment of her was unsatisfactory, and she intended to bring it to a stop should the relationship become more serious.

Jo had read enough romance novels to know that when the hero kissed the heroine, it rendered her incoherent. Authors wrote volumes about heat spreading through the woman's body and her inability to form rational thoughts. The problem with these descriptions was that the hero devoured the heroine's lips, but Chase only ever kissed her on the cheek. While she was unskilled in matters of the heart, this cheek kissing didn't seem reasonable in a relationship that would lead to a commitment.

Jo had only one sibling, her sister Hope. As they became teenagers, Hope dated various men until she met her Mr Right three years after starting work. Jo and Hope were very different, and although her sister encouraged her, Jo rarely had the confidence to put herself out there. With no close friends to discuss this cheek-kissing problem with, Jo wondered if she should ask her sister, but her embarrassment stopped her from doing so. What would Hope say if Jo confided in her?

Chapter Three

Jo was glowing, and her weight loss showed in the dress's fit. An almost-starvation diet had resulted in the loss of 30 kilos. Her legs no longer resembled tree trunks, and the cleavage at the top of her dress showcased smaller breasts. Sure, she was still overweight, but Chase didn't appear to mind.

"Are you ready to go?" her sister, Hope, asked.

Jo gave her a beaming smile. "I am. Can you believe this? A handsome, charming man is marrying me today! Can you imagine that?"

Hope smiled at her. She had met Chase and couldn't fault his behaviour when he accompanied Jo to their home for dinner, but she felt there was an ulterior motive behind the well-mannered façade of Jo's fiancé. Sisters should support each other, but Hope had doubts regarding this wedding. She could never agree that this wedding was a fairy tale and worried it might all fall apart.

"We need to go; we don't want Chase to think you've left him at the altar."

The day was everything Jo had hoped. The wedding service was brief, and the kiss Chase gave her was chaste but sweet. That sweet kiss warmed her insides, and she was eager for the guests to leave so they could start their honeymoon. Chase was never demonstrative in public. Jo didn't mind his lack of public affection because being together made them the centre of attention as women wondered how a fat chick had scored the hot guy.

The wedding venue was at a swanky resort that Chase had his heart set on from the first discussion of wedding venues. Jo was happy to fund the wedding because she intended this to be a once-in-a-lifetime event. With so few friends of her own, Chase's friends comprised the guest list. Jo recognised some of the men who accompanied him the night she and Chase first met, and she admitted to herself that she didn't like the supercilious way his friends spoke to her. Jo hoped that, now that Chase was married and no longer visiting bars to drink with his friends, she would see little of the group. Much to her dismay, Chase's mates hung on after the other guests left.

"My friends might be here for a while longer. Why don't you go to our room and prepare for bed? I'll be up soon." Chase gave her a peck on the cheek and patted her on the bottom when she turned to leave. After showering and putting on a nightgown, Jo hoped her new husband liked it; she sat and waited for him to arrive. With each passing hour, her excitement and anticipation turned to despair. What could keep a groom from his bride on their wedding night? Shouldn't Chase leave his mates to celebrate on their own? Were his mates always going to come before her needs?

Eventually, she heard a stumbling step in the hallway outside, and she braced herself as the doorknob turned. Chase walked into the room, a broad smile on his handsome face.

"Sorry, but the boys wanted to celebrate my good fortune," he slurred.

"Are you coming to bed?" Jo asked.

"You betcha."

As Chase tried to remove his shirt, Jo watched his ineffectual efforts. After removing his shirt, he fell while trying to take off his trousers. She walked to his side of the bed to help.

"Sit, and I can help."

Chase leered at her. "Eager to get me out of my pants, are you?" When Chase conceded and sat on the bed, Jo removed his shoes and socks and undid his belt. With his button and zip undone, she said, "Raise your hips so I can slide these off you."

After shaking out Chase's pants and hanging them over a chair, she took a deep breath. Fat girls never had offers from boys, so this would be a first for her. Turning back to the bed, she saw Chase stretched across the bed, dead to the world. As her mouth gaped and her eyes glazed with unshed tears, he released a slight snore and rolled over. Tonight was her wedding night, and her groom had passed out on the bed. Humiliation gave her a sick sensation. How dare he do this to her?

Uncertainty assailed her. Should she try to shove Chase over so she could climb into bed, or should she give up and sleep in the other room? Jo swore to herself as she pushed Chase; he rolled away from her, and the space he vacated allowed her to climb into the bed. During the night, the sound of someone vomiting and dry retching woke Jo. Knowing it was mean and spiteful didn't stop her from feeling pleased with this outcome. Chase had humiliated her, and now he had to pay for it. When the bathroom light turned off, she held her breath.

"Josephine, are you awake?"

"Yes."

"It's better if I sleep in the other room for the rest of the night. I'm sorry, tonight hasn't turned out as I'd expected. Goodnight."

Bitter disappointment slammed into her. Would Chase rectify the situation in the morning? Not only had she not had a proper wedding night, but she also had to sleep alone. Chase's snoring kept her awake until the early hours of the morning. Exhaustion from the hectic day before overtook Jo, and she fell into a restless sleep.

The light was peeking through the curtains when the door closed, waking her. She rolled over and closed her eyes, lying in bed as she remembered the farce that had been her wedding night. It would serve Chase right if he had to wait on her before he could have breakfast or take one of the many tours the resort offered.

Jo lay in bed, trying to decide what to do. Did she rise and go downstairs to join Chase, or should she take her time and make him wait for her? She dozed for a while and then took a leisurely bath before dressing, ready for the day. It surprised her that Chase hadn't returned to the room to get her for breakfast, but she pushed the thought away as she headed for the lift. Jo noted the lack of guests and food when she entered the dining room. She glanced at her wristwatch, verifying the time; breakfast should still be available. She headed to the reception desk with a groan to see if breakfast was elsewhere today. The receptionist glanced up from her computer.

"Can I help you?"

"Yes. My schedule says breakfast is available until nine-thirty, and as it is only nine o'clock now, I wondered where the meal was?"

"What room are you in, miss?"

"It's Mrs., and I'm in the honeymoon suite."

The clerk checked her computer and clicked with her mouse while Jo tapped her fingers against her thigh.

"Hm, there's a note from Mr Donaldson saying he didn't need meals today or tomorrow." The woman looked up from her computer. "As our next tour group isn't arriving for a few days, we've offered the chef and the wait staff time off. There is no one here to prepare your meal. I'm sorry."

Jo stared at the receptionist, her mouth agape.

"You are telling me that because my husband has decided that he does not need to eat, you assumed I wanted to go without food, too?"

The woman behind the counter shrugged. "We assumed you would go with your husband."

Attempting to rein in her temper, she plastered a smile on her face and said, "Can you tell me where my husband went?"

"He and his friends booked an overnight deep-sea fishing tour. They should be back before dinner tomorrow."

Could her honeymoon get any worse? Chase had abandoned her. They should have taken the time to get to know each other better and spend time alone. While her thoughts distracted her, she realised the office girl was smirking at her.

If she lost her temper, it would only make the woman's grin larger, so Jo used a tool she seldom employed. She drew herself to her full height and eyed the woman with disdain.

"You might find this entertaining, but look at the name on the credit card that paid for this charade. I expect you'll work out that it's me paying the bills, and there will be no more cash from me. I'll follow that up with a lousy report to my friends, who will inquire about my satisfaction. Call me a taxi; I will collect my bag and be straight back."

The red-faced woman sputtered. "Ah, I can, ah, we can. We can offer a driver and a limousine for your use."

Jo gave a quick laugh. "Ha! What fool would take a limo to pick up fast food? A taxi will be fine, thanks."

When she returned from her drive, there were enough bags of food to see her through the next two uncatered days. Although the resort had a swimming pool and numerous beauty and spa facilities, Jo was too insecure to remove her clothes in front of others. While Chase said her inner beauty drew him to her, she still felt self-conscious. As she flung her purse onto the lounge in the suite, she scanned the rooms that were now her jail.

She began eating as she clicked on one of the ever-present reality shows. As the show continued, she became absorbed in the dramas that disrupted the contestants' lives. When the credits rolled onto the screen, most of the food she had purchased for the next two days was gone. Jo hung her head and cried. She had worked hard to lose the kilos she had shed before her wedding, and now, she had just added all the lost weight and more. Comfort eating was an ingrained practice in her life, one she didn't rectify until she met Chase. Why was he avoiding her? What did she do to earn the lack of regard Chase showed her? Was he gay? He laughed when she suggested it, but was that why he hadn't consummated the marriage? The questions continued to roll around in her head, and the reality of her predicament was depressing.

What could a person do alone in a town when they didn't know their way around? Jo wasn't into exercise, and she didn't enjoy window shopping. What could she do? Jo rang the desk and asked the haughty woman to find her a driver and a vehicle. She planned to visit the largest bookshop in town to purchase all the titles that had captured her interest.

Later, with the couch covered in various books, Jo put her feet on the coffee table and opened the first title. The day passed as she became engrossed in the story of an unlikely heroine coming to the rescue of an entire town. When her eyes ached, Jo realised it was well after ten o'clock. With no reason to wait up, she retired for the night.

As she lay in bed, she wondered what Chase would say to her when he returned the next day. Anger warred with anguish as she looked back on what had so far happened on her honeymoon. Who in their right mind entertained their mates during the honeymoon period? When Chase surfaced, Jo intended to scold him for his behaviour. She had news for him if he believed this was how this marriage worked.

Chapter Four

The following morning, Jo called the desk and arranged for a driver. After directing the driver to a restaurant for breakfast, she intended to indulge in a movie fest. If Chase spent time with his buddies and neglected her, then Jo intended to do her own thing. She resolved not to mope and be the victim.

While Chase caught fish, she would catch up on all the new films at the local cinema. When her wayward husband returned, she would force him to sit and talk to her; pleased with this arrangement, she would tuck into a hearty breakfast before being deposited outside the twin cinemas in town.

It was dark when Jo exited the theatre. She was hungry and felt hungover; a movie fest was hard work. Jo had seen five films during the day, with a brief lunch break between the second and third films. She strolled across the road and hired a driver when she saw the taxi rank. Once Jo arrived at the resort, she resolved to talk with Chase. His behaviour towards her had been uncalled for, and she had no intention of playing second best to his mates for the entirety of their married life. The lack of a sex life was a dilemma that Jo didn't have the experience to remedy, but the romance books she read offered some suggestions. She wasn't sure if she could seduce Chase, but it might be worth trying.

She smiled at the receptionist when she entered the resort's foyer and continued to her apartment. The tidy rooms she left earlier that day were now unrecognisable. Wet, smelly clothes lay strewn across the floor, and a duffel that Chase must have used on his fishing trip lay open on the carpet. The duffel's contents spilled out of the unzipped opening, further adding to the room's disarray.

Once she skirted around the piles of clothes, she shoved open the door of Chase's room. Several pairs of trousers and shirts lay across the bed, but there was no sign of her husband. After a cursory check through the rest of the suite, she realised Chase was not there. Jo dialled the reception desk.

"Reception? How can I help you?"

"This is Mrs Donaldson. As you appear to know more of my husband's whereabouts than I do, please tell me where I might find him?"

"Ah, Mr Donaldson went out with a group of friends. They were going somewhere for dinner."

Jo closed her eyes for a moment. Pain exploded in her chest, and she thought she had suffered a heart attack for a minute.

"Mrs Donaldson?" the receptionist inquired.

Jo pulled herself together and asked, "Did they take a taxi, or did you offer a limo and driver?"

"Mr Donaldson and his friends used the limo."

"Is the driver still at the resort?"

"Ah, yes. The driver returned a while ago but has to pick up the group at eleven-thirty."

"Fine, ask the driver to meet me in the foyer in fifteen minutes. Please send housekeeping to my room if it's not too much trouble."

After organising for the housekeeper to take all the dirty clothes and restore the room, she headed to the lobby. The driver leaned against the reception desk but stood as she arrived.

"Good evening, Mrs Donaldson. Where can I take you?"

"Nowhere at the moment, but I have questions to ask you. Can we move to a more secluded spot?"

The driver said, "Let's go to the resort staffroom. No one is there now, so we won't be disturbed."

Jo followed the driver through a series of corridors that led to the staffroom. "What questions can I answer for you?"

"My husband is Chase Donaldson. Where did you take him and his buddies?"

"I took them to the new nightclub called The Meeting Place. It's in the city's heart."

"Did they have women with them?"

"Ah, yeah. Four young women were on the fishing trip, and they accompanied the men."

"I have to ask this, although it may sound tacky to you. Were the women paired with the men or accompanying them?"

The driver ran his hand across the back of his neck. His face flushed, and he averted his eyes. From his body language, Jo knew what the answer was. The driver glanced at her. "I'm sorry, ma'am, but each woman was with a man."

She closed her eyes and swayed. A firm hand steadied her, and she found herself seated in a large recliner. Chase's lofty words about loving her kind heart and fun personality sounded good. So, the bastard wasn't gay. Why did he marry her? What was in it for him?

"Thank you for answering those questions. My husband isn't the man I thought I was marrying. Can we return to the reception area? I have details to change."

With her bags packed, Jo made her way to the foyer. She paid the bill for two additional days and informed the receptionist that she would not be paying Chase's bills after that. In twelve hours, she intended to cancel his credit card, and the receptionist would be unpaid if she assumed it was still valid.

Chase might think he was dealing with a simpleton, but Jo was no easy mark, having been taken advantage of by people for her wealth over the years. While she didn't flash around her money, those close to her knew she was worth millions. Her father had bequeathed a substantial amount to Hope, her step-sister, who had no business interests. Her deceased father had built a business that provided the family with a comfortable lifestyle, and when he died, she inherited his business empire. Managers ran most of the companies Jo oversaw, but she kept a close eye on them through regular meetings.

Jo declined the driver's offer to transport her to another motel. She pointed out that he might feel obliged to answer his questions if he drove her elsewhere, and Chase inquired about her whereabouts. The driver bowed in understanding. When the taxi arrived, the kind man loaded her bags and stood to watch as the cab drove away. He shook his head as he walked back to the reception desk. "What a bastard act. I've seen slimeballs before, but this one takes the cake. What man runs around on his honeymoon as though he were unmarried?"

"Come off it, Tom. How could a woman like her think she could constrain a man like that?"

"What do you mean, a woman like her, and a man like that?"

"Do you have blinkers on, Tom? She's fat, obese even, and he's hot. Nobody would see those two as a couple."

"So you're saying that because she is fat, she has no feelings, and he can do what he wants?"

"No, she is distraught at the moment because he is acting as if he is still single, but if she presumed she could shackle him, then she is delusional."

The driver, Tom, shook his head and walked away.

Chapter Five

The taxi dropped Jo off at the front of the single-story motel. The motel suited her for two reasons: first, its proximity to the airport. She intended to fly out in the morning, so she preferred to be close to the airport. She had a second good reason for choosing the motel. If Chase came looking for her, he would try the top-end establishments he preferred, rather than the inexpensive ones she frequented.

It was a long night, with nothing but her thoughts to keep her company. Her mind kept rehashing the same question: why did Chase marry her if he had no interest in building their relationship? He showed her consideration and affection when they were together. True, they didn't progress beyond kisses on the cheeks and hugs in their physical connection, but Chase said he wanted their wedding night to be unique. Well, his wish came true; the wedding night was unforgettable. Tears flowed as she remembered how charming he had been, and then he changed into an insensitive, selfish swine once the ceremony ended.

When morning arrived, Jo felt exhausted and resentful. Last night, she had turned off her mobile, but now, on the off chance that her errant husband called, she turned it back on and checked the screen. There were no missed calls; she wondered if Chase realised she had left.

The trip to the terminal was short and completed with the help of the airport shuttle. Jo joined the other travellers and recalled her excitement when she landed. Now, there was nothing but bitter disappointment and crushed dreams. When Suzanne said, "Think you're smart snagging a hottie tonight? Trust me, he may have wanted to chat this evening, but he's way out of your league. You'd best forget him. Hot guys don't go out with fat chicks," she had only spoken the truth.

Jo pulled out a book, and as she did, she noticed the elegant engagement ring and its partner, her wedding band. She wanted to throw them both at Chase, but satisfied herself with wrenching them off and throwing them into her handbag. She most assuredly paid for both rings, considering she opened a credit card in Chance's name. That credit card would cease to exist in a few hours, and his easy access to her money would go with it.

When she arrived home, her head throbbed, and her body ached. She wanted to call her sister to unburden herself of her problems, but felt too embarrassed to tell anyone else what a fiasco her honeymoon had been.

However, one thing she could do was cancel Chase's credit card. If he didn't want to act like a husband, she didn't intend to treat him like one. The call centre that Jo rang was helpful. As the primary cardholder, she could close the credit card, and after reporting it as stolen, the call centre shut it down immediately. How fast would Chase return when he realised he had to pay for his purchases?

Jo ordered a pizza, and when the driver arrived with her food, she retired to the couch and her favourite reality TV show. She ignored the phone when it rang and let it go to voicemail. The message was brief: "Pick up, Josephine; I need to talk to you!" The phone rang four more times during the evening, and she ignored each one. "Well, it sucks to be you," she thought. She decided he needed to come back here if he wanted to talk.

Once she retired for the night, she turned off the ringing phone. Her grief was still like a blow to the heart, but mixed with growing anger and sadness. How dare he ring her, and how dare he demand she 'pick up'? As Chase hadn't found the interest to consummate the marriage, she intended to ring her solicitor to start proceedings to have the marriage annulled tomorrow. Soon, he would find out who controlled the purse strings.

Chase has spent months charming her, and while she thought he spent too much time with his mates, she never doubted his commitment after that first aborted date. Who spends months convincing someone that they are charming and devoted, only to throw that out the window once they sign the marriage license? Chase may have deceived her into believing he cared for her, but his motives baffled Jo. What did he have to gain from the marriage? Sure, she bankrolled him for the last week or two, but a wealthy wife was not a motive to marry. Unfortunately, it was probably his reason for marrying. He knew she was rich, but she kept the extent of her wealth a secret. Did he hope to stay married long enough to have half of her possessions? It was a problem Jo needed to share with someone, but shame kept her silent.

Jo rolled over. Tonight, she aimed to sleep; tomorrow, she might need her wits about her.

Chapter Six

The noise of the key in the door warned Jo of Chase's presence. His use of the key, given in good faith, angered her.

"Josephine, where are you?"

As she walked out of the kitchen, she glowered at Chase.

"I am here, but I wonder what you are doing here. Did you run out of playmates?"

"Don't be smart. You cut off the credit card."

"I reported the card stolen; the bank cancelled the card."

"Why the hell did you do that? You knew I had the card."

"When I got that card, it was for my husband, but as you didn't want to be him, I revoked it."

"What do you mean?"

Jo let out a brief snort. "After the service, you got so drunk that you couldn't perform on our wedding night. After telling the receptionist not to worry about food, you went fishing for two days. The stupid woman assumed we'd go together as it was our honeymoon, so the resort provided no food for two days. To top it off, you escorted some tart to a nightclub. Did you score that night, 'cause I sure didn't?"

From his expression, Chase realised he had pushed her too far. He hadn't thought past the ceremony. It never occurred to him that marriage would impede his movements. The embarrassment of having the credit card declined rankled, and anger surged in his throat.

"You didn't consider talking about your dissatisfaction before you cut off the card?"

"Chase, you are an imbecile. When could I speak to you? The only time we spent together was the wedding night when you passed out on the bed and later vomited."

Chase had the decency to look embarrassed.

"Sorry, I've never been able to do what I want; money always has been a hindrance. When I realised that the resort offered deep-sea fishing, I couldn't resist. Let's pretend the last week didn't happen and move on."

"Should we forget you were unfaithful on your honeymoon? The only person you should have bedded was me, not some skank you picked up on the fishing trip."

Chase's face flushed an ugly shade of red, and his lips tightened.

Jo took some pleasure in watching him scramble for excuses. The question was, would he honour his end of the bargain this time?

Chase moved closer to her. "Why don't you climb into bed? I'll be up in a few minutes. We need to have our wedding night again."

Jo hesitated. While she wanted Chase to make love to her, it didn't change his appalling behaviour at the resort. What happened after he bedded her? Would he go on his merry way, picking up girls and hanging out with his mates? Was he going to ignore her after this night, only coming to heel when she cut off his funds? Damn, she didn't know what to do. She remembered that he had once taken her for a fool; was she prepared to let him do it again?

Jo walked toward the bedroom, unsure she was doing the right thing. Her tummy somersaulted, and the blush on her face rose from her breasts to her eyebrows. The romance novels had surely exaggerated, but this would be the best experience of her life if they were even partially correct. Now, she would understand what it was like to be with a man.

Chase walked into the bedroom a few minutes later, and she nearly swooned. He wore no shirt, and the broad expanse of skin across his well-defined shoulders and chest was on display. A tattoo circled powerful arm muscles, and the light chest hairs snaked towards the waistband of black dress pants. Her pulse raced, and her fingers ached to touch his naked skin.

"Ah, Chase, I have never done this before."

Chase gazed at her, surprise wreathing his face.

"Oh, okay. Leave this up to me. It will be fine."

Chase turned out the lights, and anticipation filled her as he lowered himself onto the bed. The blackout curtains made the room pitch dark without the lights, and Jo found it disturbing that she couldn't see the man who was to make love to her. Even though Jo didn't want him to see her, she would have preferred to look at his well-toned body. The light touches and fleeting kisses did nothing to fire up her blood, and when she heard the crinkle of a foil packet, she wondered what Chase was doing. He smeared her vagina and clit with freezing lube and forced himself into her. The pain of his invasion made her cry out, and he hesitated before plunging into her again. After grunting a few times, Chase rolled off her and climbed out of bed to dispose of the condom.

When he left the bed, Jo lay curled up in a ball. Her body felt bruised, and tears rolled down her cheeks. The damned romance books didn't talk about the pain, the embarrassment, or the mess. The books spoke of fiery kisses and loving caresses, but she had encountered nothing like that. Chase had pecked her mouth and spent a short time on each breast. She felt violated, not loved. If this was what intimacy was, the fewer times Chase wanted to do it, the better. Looking back on the honeymoon, Jo was glad Chase hadn't done that on the first night.

Chapter Seven

After the night Chase consummated their marriage, Jo could barely bring herself to look at her husband. It didn't take a genius to know that he wouldn't inflict such pain on a regular girlfriend, because he wouldn't draw women in droves if he did. Whether she should continue this farce of a marriage plagued her during the day and kept her awake at night. Her infatuation with the man she thought she had married died a little more each day.

As they settled into a routine, Chase found endless excuses to leave the house or to avoid coming home. Chase hadn't visited her bed since the first time, and she was relieved but wondered if it might be better the second time. She contemplated asking her sister Hope about her experience in bed with her husband, but embarrassment kept her quiet.

Chase left the house in the morning when she arose. The place always looked immaculate, and she wondered if he slept in the bed or returned early each morning to support the illusion. Curiosity prompted her to check the room Chase used, citing difficulties sleeping with someone else as her excuse. Chase attended meetings and workshops late at night, and Jo didn't understand why a car dealer needed to work late. He said that people who bought luxury cars preferred to view their prospective purchases in the privacy of their own homes, so he drove the vehicles to their homes.

Marriage was nothing as Jo envisaged. She was still lonely, and her eating disorder resurfaced. Left to herself each evening, she took refuge in reality shows and food. While watching an hour-long show, she could demolish two packets of biscuits, a tub of ice cream, or two or three blocks of chocolate. Her weight ballooned, and she felt miserable. The increased weight made it harder for her to get around and made her an easy target for teasing and bullying at work.

When the sniggering at work began, she wondered why her workmates were being mean. Fat people often found themselves the butt of jokes, but the attention she was receiving was hostile. Jo tried to keep her head up and do her best job. She caught the end of quick conversations and whispered comments as the days passed. What was everyone discussing?

She spent the lunch break alone or at her desk. The other women flooded back in, laughing and talking, and she felt even more despondent. One Friday afternoon, Jo left her office before the others returned and locked herself in a restroom cubicle. If she remained there for a while, it would spare her the grins and smirks of her coworkers. As she prepared to leave the cubicle, noises outside the door forewarned her of someone else in the room. When the door opened, she retreated before the women spotted her. Suzanne and her best friend, Carole, walked into the room.

"I wonder where fat Jo is? She's normally at her desk, but it was vacant when we came in." A tittering laugh punctuated Suzanne's remark.

"I can't decide if she is stupid or just pathetic. How can she not know her husband is cheating on her? He's always with Kelly when he goes out. I wouldn't mind offering to help him work off his frustrations," laughed Carole.

"Yeah, I told her hot guys like him didn't go for fat girls. He married her for her money."

Carole cast a doubtful look at her friend. "Money? What money? She doesn't look like she has two cents to rub together."

"I'm not sure. Someone told me Jo has buckets of money."

The voices faded as the two women left the restroom. Jo sat on a pedestal, her face white as a ghost. Her hand shook, and her stomach knotted. Chase was cheating on her, and the entire building knew. Is it any wonder they were snickering and making comments?

When she returned home that night, her cheeks burned from the more apparent comments floating around the office. What did she do now? The urge to ring Chase's phone overwhelmed her. As she dialled his number, she prayed he would answer. A female voice answered. The background noise was deafening; it was the sound of music and bar chatter. Jo hung up the phone; she didn't want Chase to devise a pathetic excuse for why Kelly answered his phone. Although it was still early, she considered going to bed. What were the other options? Television was an option, but tonight, she thought her life was more tragic than the reality shows. She recalled the barbs from her workmates. Did Chase marry her for money? How long did a person have to remain married before the spouse could claim half of their partner's wealth?

As she stood to leave the kitchen, her cell phone rang. She didn't want to talk to anyone. Her phone beeped, displaying a message. When she glanced at it, she realised the call was from her lawyer. What to do? Should she call him back or leave it till the morning? What the hell? It wasn't as if she had anything important to do

"Barry, hello, it's Jo. You wanted to speak?"

"Ah, I'm glad you called back. I didn't want to call you at work, but I must discuss your PR business. There's a buyer interested, and you said you wanted to offload it. If you want to sell the business, we need to meet to work out an exit strategy and a price for the business."

The announcement momentarily stunned her. She recalled all the ridicule and mockery she had faced from the workers at the PR company she owned. Her fellow employees and the boss, Mr Rogers, didn't know that the business was one of her many interests in the city. She had earned her job at the firm not because she owned the company, but because of her skill level. She had considered shedding the business for a while. With the company's work environment becoming toxic, she intended to leave.

"Barry, that's an excellent idea. I'll take tomorrow off, and we can meet. Does that suit you?"

With the news from the phone call, Jo realised she needed to make decisions regarding her assets and her wayward husband. When the knock on the door came, she checked her watch—the early night appeared to be a thing of the past. She walked to the door and opened it, revealing her sister.

"Hope, what are you doing here?"

"Can I come in rather than conduct an extended conversation in the entry hall?"

"Oh, sure. This visit is unexpected. What brings you here?"

Hope took a seat and looked at her lap. She fiddled with her earrings for a moment or two before she spoke.

"This is hard to say, but I heard rumours about Chase playing away. When Glen and I ate out tonight, we saw the evidence to go with the talk. His companion was a beautiful woman, and they were not just friends. Did you know about this?"

Jo took a deep, quivering breath to steady herself and nodded at her sister. The fiasco of the honeymoon and Chase's countless nights away came pouring out, accompanied by many tears.

"The women at work have been laughing and talking about me for the last month. Everyone at work knows the truth, and I was the only stupid person who didn't." Tears tracked down her face, her misery evident in her eyes.

Hope patted Jo on the arm. "I have an indelicate question to ask. As Chase spent all his time on your honeymoon with his mates, did you, ah....?"

"Consummate the marriage, you mean?"

"Yes, did you?"

Jo shuddered. "Yes, and I don't know why romance novels always talk about the passionate kisses and the erotic touches and the blissful ending. It was embarrassing, messy, and painful. I had no earth-shattering high at the end; Chase got off the bed and walked away. Thank God he only wanted to do it once."

"Oh, no, Jo, that is not how it should happen. If he loved you and you loved him, it would be different. What are you going to do now?"

"I don't know; I suppose I get rid of him. He said he was interested in me, and I was stupid enough to believe that. My only concern is how he will react when he finds out his cash cow has deserted him. When I realised what he and his mates were up to during the honeymoon, I cancelled his credit card. He sent aggressive voicemails and got pretty hostile when he returned here. I'm a bit frightened of him."

Hope stared into space, and Jo knew this was her way of thinking. When her sister smiled, Jo felt a sense of relief; Hope had devised a plan.

"The way to avoid his hostility is to wrap everything up and leave town before he realises you're gone. You must get him out of the house for four or five days."

Jo thought and said, "What if I reinstate his credit card and tell him he can't come home for four or five days, so he should stay in a motel? Um, I could say I'm having the house painted. He and that skank will run up huge bills, but it would be worth it if I can empty the house and put it on the market before he realises."

Hope laughed. "Good strategy, sis. If you pay off that expensive car and leave money in the joint account, it will take longer to notice you are missing."

With a plan to execute, Jo felt relief for the first time in weeks.

Chapter Eight

After Hope left, Jo felt more confident, despite a thumping headache. Crying about her situation didn't make her feel any better, so she tried to put her heartbreak aside until she sorted out her life. The sisters had made a to-do list, and Hope had offered to help with some of the tasks. The first task was to ensure Chase didn't return to the house for the next few days. When she rang Chase's phone, Kelly answered it, which didn't surprise her.

"Hi, this is Chase's phone. Can I help you?"

"Yes, I want to speak to my husband. Put him on the phone, thanks."

There was a muted conversation between Chase and Kelly, and then Chase said,

"Hi, darl. What can I do for you?"

"Well, you might come home occasionally, and if you stopped making a spectacle of yourself in public with that slut, you're screwing, I would appreciate it."

There was dead silence at the other end of the phone; Jo laughed. "What, you thought fat ladies don't hear gossip and don't have thousands of bitchy women waiting to repeat what they saw?"

"You don't understand. Kelly and I are friends, and as we work together, we often see each other. I didn't mean to ignore you. It's just that we've been flat out at work. I'll come home early tonight."

"Well, wouldn't that be something? You've been flat-out, but I doubt it is related to work. It's an interesting strategy to work out of bars and nightclubs. Do you drum up much business with singles and drunks? Don't bother coming back for the next three or four days; I'm having the house painted. I'm not sure how long the painters will be here. Drop sheets will be placed in all the rooms, so you won't be able to access the house. Stay at a motel and use your credit card to cover the expenses. I'll let you know when you can return.

Jo was sure that Chase would use this opportunity to live it up big in one of the more prestigious motels in town. He would not consider returning now that she had given him a free pass. She worked on the jobs that she and Hope had listed. The primary task was to close and move her bank accounts away from the bank she had frequented for years. The joint account, which Chase regularly accessed for withdrawals, had $10,000, and Jo paid out for his flash imported car. Those two measures would give her breathing space before he realised something was happening.

While Jo sorted through personal tasks, Hope contacted a charity and informed them that her sister had donated all the linen, bedding, kitchen utensils, and crockery they could pack in one day—the furniture she would place in storage as soon as the property was sold.

Jo postponed her meeting with the lawyer while she reorganised her life. Any excess money not needed for the day-to-day operations of the businesses went into her bank account in the Cayman Islands. "Get at that," she taunted Chase.

Once the charity had collected its windfall, Jo was ready to put the house on the market. She ensured that Chase's bedroom remained untouched and then called a real estate agent to obtain an estimate and initiate the process.

"Trudy, I have stipulations about who you show the house to. I don't want a for-sale sign on the property. There will be no stickybeaks, and the people you show through the house need to have photo IDs so that you know who they are. The other stipulation is that anyone who wants to view the house must prove they can afford to buy the property. I don't care if they offer a letter from their bank to state that the money will be forthcoming or whether they show you their bank account balance."

Trudy, the real estate agent, nodded in agreement, but there was a query in her eyes.

"That's unusual. Is there a reason for these requirements?"

"Yes. I don't want you to show it to anyone who might help my husband move back into the house. The house is mine, but it might be tough to get him to budge if he moves back in. I do not want my husband and his girlfriend on the property. I have a photo of them, so ensure the keys are secure and they don't gain access."

When Jo finally reached her lawyer's office, she ran through the steps she had taken after giving him the lowdown on the marriage.

"These days, irretrievable differences are the reason for most divorces, but in this case, we might have photo evidence as leverage. I have a bloke I use sometimes, and if you can point him in the right direction, he will help."

Jo pulled out her mobile. After keying in the number she wanted, she waited a few moments before someone answered the phone.

"Good morning, Hilderbrand and Rowdone prestige cars. How may I help you?"

"Good morning. I was hoping to talk to Chase Donaldson. Is he in today?"

"I'm sorry, Mr Donaldson had to take emergency leave. He will be back next week."

Jo screwed up her face and rolled her eyes. "I'm sorry to hear that. Can I do anything to help? We are good friends."

The receptionist lowered her voice and confided, "He has a problem with his wife. She has alcohol use disorder and has gone off the wagon, and he is trying to help dry her out."

Jo barely managed a civil goodbye. She jumped to her feet and yelled, "Did you hear what she said? An alcoholic, am I? The bastard! Not only is he a lying scumbag, but he's blackening my reputation. Set your bloke on him; tell him to start in the most expensive motel in town."

Barry, the solicitor, shook his head in disgust.

"What do you want to do with the offer from the buyer for your One-Stop PR business?"

While she and Barry discussed the other firm's offer, Jo's resolve to pay back her workmates hardened.

"The new owners intend to amalgamate One-Stop and their business, right?"

"Yes. There will be job losses as the other company restructures. Is that a problem for you?"

"Hell, no. I want the meeting at work. I want those bitches to suffer; they deserve strife after what they've put me through every day of my working life. I want to tell them that their jobs are in jeopardy."

Jo completed the jobs she and Hope had listed to prepare for the meeting. A locksmith changed the outside locks on the doors, and she sent a new key to the real estate agent. The worker secured the door from the garage with padlocks on the home side of the door, so, short of using an axe, no one could access the house from the garage. She purposely didn't change the code on the garage so that when Chase tried to put his car away, the boxes of his belongings and the furniture from his room impeded his entry. Happy with her progress, Jo anticipated the business meeting with glee.

Dressed in a business suit, Jo made her way to work. When she arrived, the place was in an uproar.

"What's happening?" she asked the women congregating in the hallway.

"Another company is taking us over. There's a meeting with the owner and a solicitor in half an hour to tell us what will happen to us."

"What do you mean, what will happen to us?" Jo asked.

"Well, the other company will let workers go. We believe a new owner will retain the best workers, but some staff members may lose their jobs. I'd be worried; fat, lazy chicks will be first to go."

"Is that so?"

She had felt guilty when she viewed the chaos in the hallway, but Jo's sympathy disappeared as other women agreed.

Jo sat in a chair at the front as the workforce gathered in the conference room. When her boss, Mr Rogers, arrived, he glared at her. "I don't think it's proper for you to sit at the front, Mrs Donaldson. Please move to the back; we don't want to give the owner the impression that you are our most valued worker. If we're lucky, the owner may not notice you back there."

"Why am I hiding?"

Barry walked into the room, and Mr Rogers shot forward to greet him.

"Mr Anthony, I assume? Will the owner be attending?"

Barry put his hand out to shake Mr Roger's hand and said,

"Yes, the boss will be here. We can start while we're waiting." As Barry outlined the sale of the business and the other company's intention to amalgamate the two firms, Jo could see the concern on the faces of her workmates. The bitchy women who had spent a long time bullying her looked calm and confident.

When Barry finished his spiel, he asked if there were questions. The first question was, who would choose the workers who had to leave? Barry smiled. "The owner should answer that question." He smiled at Jo as she stood. Mr Rogers snarled at her as she rose from her seat.

"Mrs Donaldson, you must stay in place until Mr Anthony introduces the boss."

"Mr Rogers, I don't believe I need an introduction. You may be the first person I suggest to the new owner to fire. Take a seat; you're holding up proceedings."

The gaping mouths of her workmates were a pleasant sight, and Jo grinned at Barry as she sat beside him. She looked at her colleagues and smiled.

"As the owner of this business, the decision to sell was an easy one for me. The toxic atmosphere that has grown under the present management makes me no longer want to be associated with this company. My recommendation to the new owners will play a significant role in determining who keeps their jobs. A few of you may as well pack your desks straight away. You know who you are: the people who pretend to work while hanging around the copier gossiping, the individuals who give their work to a subordinate. Also, the bitches who have discussed my marriage endlessly to the cheating, lying scumbag I married. You can also pack your bags if you have ever made disparaging comments about how fat I am. Any more questions?"

Stunned silence greeted Jo's speech. "No questions?' We're almost finished for now. I have a list of people I'd like to stay here for a while. If I don't call your name, you can leave."

Barry handed her the list, and she called out the names of twelve people. The rest of the workforce left, and the chosen twelve sat rigidly in their seats. Fear marked their faces, so she talked as soon as the door closed behind the other workers.

"You guys are the people I suggest the new owners keep." A murmur of relief swept through the group.

"I don't intend to recommend anyone else. You have always acted professionally and often taken on tasks that others should have handled. I will warn the new owners about the other staff's work ethic and bullying tactics, so do you want me to recommend you all?"

Smiles and affirmations greeted her announcement.

"Okay, you will hear from the new owners soon, and I wish you the best of luck."

Jo looked at her solicitor and grinned. "I think we're finished here. Oh, just one thing, people. Have the day off; you won't want to put up with the bitches today. Tomorrow is a new start for you. Go home now and share the news with your families."

As she stood, Barry held out his hand. Jo gave him a high-five and laughed. "I'm rarely vindictive, but this was sweet revenge. The bitches won't get a reference, so finding another job will be more challenging."

"What are you going to do now?"

"There is nothing for me here. I packed my bags and stowed them in the car before leaving this morning. I am going to hop in the car and drive. I don't know where I'm going, but I will keep in touch. I first need to trade in my car, but I'll do that when I'm hundreds of kilometres from here. Thank you, Barry. Please don't tell Chase where I am, and push the divorce through as fast as possible."

Barry's face reddened, and he said, "I have to ask this question, even though it's personal."

"You know more about me than anyone except my sister, so ask away."

"Was the marriage consummated?"

Jo shuddered. "My sister asked the same question. The answer, unfortunately, is yes. What an embarrassing, messy, painful activity that was. Why do you ask?"

"Well, if Chase didn't consummate the marriage, we could have applied for an annulment."

"That would be easy, and considering the activity was so unpleasant, I should get time off for good behaviour."

Barry leaned over and kissed Jo on the cheek. "Stay safe", was all he said as he walked away.

Chapter Nine

When Jo's phone call came, Chase didn't answer. If he pretended not to know the house was habitable, he could stay in this swanky hotel with Kelly. Jo had told him to use his restored credit card, so he and Kelly spent lavishly. Room service delivered caviar and champagne. Kelly utilised the spa and beauty treatments, while Chase became a popular figure in the bar, earning huge tips and constant demand for beverages from his friends. He believed his sacrifice in marrying Jo entitled him to this lavish lifestyle.

Eventually, though, the credit card bill mounted, and he knew he needed to keep his wife sweet, or she might cut him off again. As he and Kelly collected their luggage, she said,

"Can you get the valet to pick us up in the garage? Whenever I go out, there's a creepy guy with a camera. I haven't seen him take any photos, but he makes me uncomfortable."

Chase laughed. "Don't stress! It will be the paparazzi. Get used to it; we'll be in the news when we're rich. The rich and famous people get noticed in the media, but we can leave from the garage if it makes you happy."

The valet handed the keys to Chase, and he settled into the seat of his luxury car. Jo was useful for something. This car was the vehicle of his dreams, and she had not even raised an eyebrow when he said he had purchased the newest model. As the engine caught, the vehicle's deep rumble made his eyes glow with pleasure. Kelly groaned with contentment, even though her patience was wearing thin.

"How soon can you make moves to end the marriage?"

Chase flicked a glance at her. "Remember that we decided on six months. So far, the marriage has survived for two months; do the math. Don't ruin a good thing because you can't show any patience. It's not as if I spend much time with the fat cow, but having spent a week in a motel, I should appear and stay the night."

"Can't we spend the night at my place?"

"No, we can't. Jo is the cash cow; if I don't spend time with her, she might cut off the credit card as she did after the honeymoon. Why are you complaining? It's I who has to spend the night with her. She is so fat that she can barely walk, and her whole body sways and jiggles each time she moves. The woman is revolting, and you get spared all of that. She is pleased to see me when I return, so let's keep it that way."

Chase dropped Kelly off at her house. Before pulling out, he checked the rearview mirror and noticed a car following behind. Was it the same car Chase saw earlier in the day? With a shrug, he made a U-turn and drove toward Jo's house.

Chase wondered why the house looked different as he drove up the driveway. It had an abandoned air, and Chase wondered at the empty look. He parked in the driveway and took a look around. Someone had closed the house's curtains, and junk mail was in the letterbox. What was happening? Where had Jo stayed while the painters were here, he wondered. He hadn't considered that while he and Kelly lived it up. Shaking his head at that sudden thought, Chase pressed the remote for the garage door and drove towards the widening gap. He swiftly applied the brakes. The garage was inaccessible to the car because of the boxes and furniture piled along the walls. What the hell? Chase thought. Was this someone's idea of a joke? As he waded through the stacks of his belongings, his bemusement turned to anger. Chase approached the door between the house and the garage with fists clenched and a scowl. Try as he may, he could not insert the key into the lock. Twisting the key, Chase cursed when it was plain that the key did not fit the lock. In frustration, he shook the door and realised there was no give in the door. Someone had attached something to the other side of the opening, and even if he smashed the lock, it looked unlikely he could enter the house.

Chase grabbed the first thing that came to hand and hurled it against the garage's brick wall. The lamp hit the ground and shattered into a thousand pieces. The rage grew as he kicked and slashed at his belongings, heedless of the fact that these were his possessions and he would need to replace them. Broken lamps, destroyed discs, and shredded clothing littered the garage floor, giving it a wasteland-like appearance.

As he surveyed the damage, Chase's anger once again raged. This mess was all Jo's fault; if she hadn't locked him out, he wouldn't have lost his cool. He ran his hands through his hair and tried to decide a course of action. He needed to stay with Kelly for the night, but how could he track Jo's solicitor to find out what was happening?

"

Chapter Ten

What do you mean she's left?" Chase yelled at Barry.

"Why don't you come to my office? We can discuss this in a civilised way. I'm free at the moment if you have the time."

Barry was ready for the showdown twenty minutes later when his secretary knocked on the door. He moved a sheaf of papers out of the way as Chase stalked into the room.

"Where the hell is my wife? What's happening?"

Barry laughed and shook his head. Pulling photos out of an envelope, he flipped through the compromising pictures of Chase.

"By the look of these, you forgot you had a wife."

Chase's face went grey as he glanced through the photographs. Kelly had been correct. Someone was watching them, but the paparazzi hadn't taken these pictures. The prints were damming, and Chase wondered how the photographer had captured so many compromising photos. There was no denying the evidence in the images, but Chase wasn't ready to give up.

"Jo and I don't share an intimate relationship, if you understand what I mean. A man needs a release; if the wife isn't interested, someone else will fill the void."

Barry shook his head. "Do you believe the rubbish you're telling me? I asked her if you consummated the marriage, and she described it as a nasty, painful, embarrassing activity."

Chase let out a choking cough. Barry tapped his pen on the photos lying on the desk. "Sounds like you can get it up for someone else, but you're an insensitive sod with your wife. No woman should describe her deflowering the way Jo did."

"Look, man, she's not exactly a sex symbol."

"Jo was overweight when you met her, and she tried hard to lose kilos before the wedding. She piled the weight back on after the debacle of a honeymoon, and because of your negligence. Tell me how many nights in full you've spent in her house?"

Chase shot up from his chair. "Listen, mate; I didn't come here to get a lecture on my behaviour. What is happening to the house, and where is Jo?"

Barry leaned back in his chair and examined Chase like a bug in a jar. "Sit down, and I will answer your questions. The house is for sale, and the real estate agent has explicit directions. You cannot access the property; if I'm not mistaken, your belongings are in the garage."

"How can she sell the house? It's my home too! She should have talked to me," Chase raged.

"The house is Jo's property, and you never lived in it. You made flying visits. She has filed for divorce and left town. The divorce papers are here with me now, but if you let me know who your solicitor is, I will forward them to him."

Chase sprang from his chair. "She can't divorce me! I won't sign the papers."

Barry glared at Chase. "Please yourself, mate, but you're not getting any substantial settlement after being married for less than two months. Jo has directed me to pay your credit card bill, and then I will cancel the card."

Chase spun around to face Barry, his face purple with rage. "The bitch! She won't get away with this. I'll fix her if she reckons she can shove me away like this."

"Mate, you've had a good run. Jo paid for that expensive status symbol you drive, and she left $10,000 in the bank account. You should be grateful that someone won't be around to repossess the car, and you have a buffer with the cash in the bank. Go back to work; stop trying to marry naïve young women for their money."

"I'll get what she owes me. As her husband, I am entitled to half of her possessions. If she believes I'll walk away for less, she is dreaming. If she doesn't put up serious cash, I'll track her down and convince her to see the error of her ways."

"The law will take a very different view regarding your entitlements after a few months of marriage, most of which you spent sleeping with your girlfriend. You've lived high on the hog for the entire time you've known Jo, and now the supposedly endless stream of money you think she has is at an end. You will be lucky to get a dollar with my photos and testimony from the resort's limousine driver. Man up and take what Jo has offered you."

As the enraged man stalked to the door, Barry was frightened for Jo. Was this guy unhinged, or was he delusional? Nobody in their right mind would consider the 'marriage' that Chase and Jo had shared entitled them to half her wealth. Chase had spent most of the nights of their marriage sleeping with his girlfriend, and according to Jo, he only came home when he wanted more money.

Jo drove through the city's outskirts, her CD blasting her favourite pop music. A sense of peace floated over her as she went. Even though she didn't have a chosen destination, her spirits rose, and she felt free and happy. Fat girls like her rarely had adventures, and Jo always tried to conform to others' expectations. She had no one else to consider, no one to give her disapproving looks or angry opinions. This trip was all for her, however long it lasted and wherever it went.

Once she cleared the city, she took the southbound lane and followed a line of other traffic as it left. Despite the music and the drive, her thoughts drifted back to Chase. How had she been so foolish as to believe a handsome man like him would be interested in her? She vowed never to allow a man to humiliate and hurt her as Chase had.

Not used to driving long distances, Jo felt tired and disoriented. Although it was time for lunch, she had no interest in food, but stopping for a drink might refresh her. Jo walked into the service station and noticed a display of locations to visit in the district. After putting her juice and pamphlets on the counter, she asked the attendant for information on the local attractions. The woman suggested places along the way that Jo might find interesting. Back in the car, Jo pored over the flyer of her interests and stopped at two of the places she had listed. Refreshed after her stop, she continued to drive. A sudden thought made her laugh. She didn't know where she was going, so she didn't need to hurry. She could stop anywhere she wanted and stay as long as she wanted. With that thought in mind, she turned off the highway onto the road that led to the waterfalls. Jo expected a breathtaking expanse of water, so it disappointed her that she couldn't see the falls from the parking lot. A walking track, graded as 'easy', accessed the falls. Three kilometres of track stretched out away from the park.

As Jo sat in the car, disappointment rushed through her. An 'easy', three-kilometre walk would not be easy for her. The sign might say it was an easy walk, but could she do it, considering her weight? She looked at her clothes. It hadn't occurred to her that her attire might hinder her during her quest. She made a snap decision, clambered out of the car, and walked around the sleek machine to open the boot. Suitcases filled the car's boot, and after rummaging around, she found jeans, a shirt, socks, and sneakers. She glanced around to ensure her privacy, then stripped to her underwear and dressed casually.

Armed with a water bottle, her mobile phone and a snack bar, Jo walked to the start of the walking trail. The trail wove its way amongst thick green foliage. Some plants looked prehistoric. Delicate, lacy leaves on palms filtered the light and threw patterns on the ground. Jo basked in the silence and beauty. Occasionally, bird calls disturbed the silence, but the sounds of the distant highway did not filter through the tranquillity of the trail.

After completing nearly a kilometre, Jo was not impressed with nature. The track climbed, and she panted from her exertions. Sweat rolled down her face and pooled under her arms. Her legs felt as heavy as logs of wood, and the fat rolls around her stomach impeded her progress. Jo looked for somewhere to sit and spied a rock not far ahead that should suffice as a seat. When she had lowered herself onto the impromptu seat, she couldn't decide: should she go on after her rest, or turn back? Where would she go after finishing here? She asked herself. The answer was wherever she wanted. With this thought in mind, she rose and continued her walk.

The path levelled out, and the walking got easier. Jo was pleased that she had persevered. As she approached a bend in the track, the sound of roaring reached her ears. The loud noise made her cringe. What was the sound? No wild animals in Australia made such a sound. Jo took a deep breath and, gathering her courage, walked around the bend.

The view that greeted her caught her breath in her throat, and her heart beat faster. Water fell from hundreds of meters above, and the flow was so fast it made the crashing sound she had heard. Bird noise was absent from this place as though the birds couldn't compete with such magnificence.

Jo roused herself, pulled out her phone, and took pictures. She knew she couldn't capture the brilliance of the falls, but the photos would remind her that she had made a three-kilometre walk and survived. She gave a small chuckle; now, she would have to endure the return trip.

Chapter Eleven

As Jo drove into Helensville, a billboard along the road advertised a health resort. Would a stint in a health resort help her lose the weight she had accumulated during her short marriage? Once in the town, Jo pulled into a park outside the newsagent's. A man at the counter smiled as she approached.

"G' day. How can I help you, miss?"

"There is no mobile phone service out here. Is there a public phone somewhere in town? I want to ring the health resort."

"That's a local call; you can use the phone here."

Jo called the resort; there had been a late cancellation, and the owner was glad to accommodate her. She thanked the newsagent and returned to her car to follow the woman's directions.

The resort was five kilometres out of town and set back from the road. As Jo drove towards the country-style building, anticipation shot through her. Could the routines and treatments at this place help her lose weight? After the walk to the falls, Jo was determined to get fit, which meant she had to lose weight.

When the owner answered the door, she scrutinised Jo.

"Come in, Miss Bromley. I'm Julie MacFarlane, the owner of this business. We offer dietary help, massage and exercise programs. If you join us, you will work predominantly with me. Leave your luggage in the car until after we talk; it might minimise what you need to bring into the house."

Jo sat in the chair the woman motioned to as they entered an office. "There is some paperwork we need to do, and then I can organise a schedule for you. What do you hope to achieve during your stay?"

"On the way here, I stopped to look at the Blackrock Falls. The walk's classification is 'easy', and I had to rest twice, so it wasn't easy. I want to walk without puffing and tie up my shoelaces by bending, not sitting and maneuvering my foot towards my hands. I want to be fitter, so I have to lose weight." Jo flushed as the woman watched her. "Too much information?" she asked.

"No. You are a remarkable woman. You didn't prevaricate; you told me precisely what you wanted."

"I need a quiet time out. My husband and I got married two and a half months ago. The gossipy bitches at work said he married me for my money. He cheated on me on the first night of the honeymoon. I'm over being sorry for myself, but I need the time to build my confidence."

"Oh, dear, you've had a rough time. I'm sure we can help."

"You can't imagine how pleased I am that someone cancelled. I might have lost my courage if I had to wait months for an appointment."

Once they completed the paperwork, Julie ran through the program she thought would help Jo.

"The program is vigorous, so sing out, and I'll change things if it gets too much. The clothes you need to bring into the house are sleepwear, exercise gear and swimmers."

"Ah, what exercise clothes do I need? I don't own togs. Once I grew up, I never went swimming, so I didn't need bathers; who wants to see a fat lady in swimmers? I can swim well, but I stopped going when my classmates joked about a whale in the pool."

Julie looked at her watch. "My afternoon is free. Why don't we make a quick trip into town? There is a store there that will have what you need. What do you say?" Jo nodded.

"Why not?"

Julie parked outside an old building. A canvas awning, a relic from the past, shaded the front window and doorway. Old-fashioned mannequins, modelling coloured clothes, decorated the front window.

As the two women entered, the doorbell chimed.

"Julie, it's lovely to see you! Have you brought me a new friend?"
Julie walked forward and hugged the other woman.

"Jo, I want you to meet a good friend, Pamela. Pam is the owner of the shop. Pam, meet Jo. She is staying with us at the retreat for a while. We need help with clothes."

"What clothes did you have in mind?"

"I need to buy workout clothes and a swimming costume. I've never done much exercise, so I don't know what I need," Jo confided to Pam.

"Well, that's why Julie brought you here. I know what you need, and we'll see if we can find something practical you agree with."

When the two women left the shop laden with bags, Jo felt happy with her shopping trip. Even though she needed to try on Pam's clothes, both women gave her feedback on her appearance. Was this how shopping with friends was supposed to feel? Jo had never been on a shopping spree, so she had no point of comparison. Who could have guessed that hopping into the car and driving could be beneficial?

Early the following day, her alarm heralded the start of her first day at the retreat. She dressed in her new workout clothes and headed to the kitchen. Four other ladies sat at the kitchen table, and a woman wearing a bright pink apron worked on a bench. When Jo walked into the kitchen, she was unsure of what to do: should she sit or make something for herself?

"Morning, dearie," said the apron-wearing woman. "I'm Mary, and I'll be preparing your breakfast soon. It helps to drink water before the meal," she said, pointing to the glasses and water jug on the table. "I'm sure these ladies can introduce themselves while you wait."

Jo poured herself a glass of water and smiled at the women at the table. "Hi, I'm Jo. Julie is helping me to become half the woman I am."

The other women smiled and introduced themselves. One woman, Toni, was halfway through her treatment and had lost twenty kilos. This news cheered Jo, and as the other women introduced themselves, they disclosed the reason for their presence at the retreat.

Jo sipped her water as the women chatted, wondering what breakfast would be like. There were no pans on the stove, no kettles boiling, no smell of toast or anything else cooking. Mary appeared busy with a blender that whirred intermittently as the women talked. When Mary approached the table, she held a tray with four enormous glasses. The contents of the glasses were different colours, so she assumed they each had different ingredients. Mary placed one in front of each of the ladies and encouraged them to begin.

Jo's concoction was pink and had a sweet, fragrant scent. When she sipped it, she was surprised by how tasty the drink was. She was still sipping it when Julie bustled through the door.

"Good morning, all. You have fifteen minutes to be at your workstations. After I fix up Jo, I will check on the rest of you."

"The woman is a whirlwind," Jo said. Toni grinned. "You have seen nothing yet, honey."

Once everyone had finished their health drinks, they went their separate ways. Julie took Jo into the gym and explained the various machines.

"I want you walking on the treadmill. You will have a twenty-minute stint, and then, after a short rest period, I will help you get set up on the bike. We have a group yoga class at eleven, and then after lunch, you can go swimming."

The schedule sounded too full, and she doubted her ability to complete Julie's planned task. Julie saw the doubt in her eyes and patted her on the shoulder.

"It will all work. Wait and see. Talk to Toni during lunch; she was in the same position as you a few weeks ago. Toni's reached her goal weight; if she stays for the full month, she will be well below her target when she leaves."

Jo gritted her teeth and approached the treadmill. The walking pace was slow, but she puffed after only a few minutes. How could she ever last twenty minutes?

"Often people find that listening to music helps," a voice behind her said. She turned her head, carefully holding the rails, and looked at Toni.

"An iPod, or your phone with music loaded and earplugs, makes the whole thing more bearable. Stop the machine, and we'll set mine up for you for today."

Touched by this woman's kindness, Jo set up the phone and earplugs for her. The twenty minutes passed more quickly when she concentrated on the music and sang along.

During her fifteen-minute break between the treadmill and the exercise bike, Toni showed Jo how to load music onto her phone. The woman searched for a spare pair of headphones and found one; Jo was now ready to listen to her own choice of music.

The time for the yoga session arrived quickly, and Jo admitted to feeling exhausted. She had never been one for exercise, and she had worked out all morning. The yoga class was not as restful as expected because the other women had advanced past the beginner stage. There were moves that Julie did not need Jo to do.

Jo gratefully sat in a chair that didn't double as exercise equipment at lunchtime. A large glass of water was obligatory before the meal. Her meal consisted of a vegetable concoction. Considering all the fluids and fibre she had consumed, she worried about how often she would need to use the bathroom. Her companions laughed and said dashes to the toilet were all the rage. Jo shook her head and giggled; at least she wouldn't be alone in the bathroom dash department.

Swimming was her favourite task that day, and Jo looked forward to spending more time in the pool as her treatment progressed. After the swim, she headed for the showers. Her legs were stiff, and her arms hurt; in fact, her entire body ached. Mixed in with her pain was a sense of achievement. The day was all but over, and she had managed the tasks without moaning or whining. They had a fish fillet, a generous serving of vegetables, and a small glass of wine for dinner; very civilised, Jo thought.

A meditation session followed the meal, and then all the residents retired to their rooms. When Jo hit the bed, she was so tired from her day of exertions that she fell asleep immediately.

Chapter Twelve

The days at the retreat flew past, and Jo increased her exercise level each day. Her only problem was the constant need to replace her clothes. Garments that fit her in the first week of her treatment no longer fit her weeks after. Pam often updated her wardrobe, and by the last week, the clothes that currently fit her more slender frame were smaller than any she had owned since her teenage years. The ladies at the retreat when Jo started had left, and new people were there. Even though the people were friendly, she never felt a connection with them as she had with the other ladies, particularly Toni.

One afternoon, towards the end of her stay, Julie entered the room, a worried frown creasing her brow.

"Jo, can I have a word with you in my office, please?"

Jo followed Julie, her anxiety growing. Why did Julie look so concerned?

"I had a phone call this morning from a man who wants to come and visit our resort. He's in town and intends to visit in an hour or two."

"Okay." Where was this conversation going?

"The problem is that he mentioned your name and said that you had recommended our retreat to him. I know you've occasionally called your solicitor, but I didn't know of any other calls you made."

Jo's stomach dropped, and she wrung her hands.

"Did you say I was here? What's his name? Oh, God, he's found me." She jumped up and said, "I must get out of here. Barry, my solicitor, told me that Chase is angry and promising retribution."

"Stop, Jo! We can hide you. When you had a tour, I didn't take you into anyone else's room, which will be the case here. I told him I didn't recognise the name when he said Josephine Bromley recommended the place."

"But my car is distinctive, and the others will say I'm here if he asks."

"We can fix all of that. Do you trust me to hide you?"

Jo nodded her head. "I still don't see how we get past the car outside and the other guests."

Making her way to the door, Julie said, "Give me a minute, and we'll sort this out."

Once Mary had driven the distinctive vehicle into the lock-up garage, the problem was solved. Julie called the other guests into the kitchen and explained the situation. Each guest agreed to avoid Chase or to pretend ignorance if pressed.

"The only place you have been in town is Pam's shop, so I'll call her."

When the sound of a car pulling up outside reached the kitchen, Julie said, "Showtime!" Jo rushed to her bedroom and locked the door. She closed the curtains for security and sat on the bed, waiting.

A few moments later, Chase knocked on the door. By peeking through the curtains, Julie could see their visitor inspecting the cars parked alongside the building. When Chase knocked on the door, Julie answered, and it surprised her that Jo's estranged husband was handsome. She smiled at him and held out her hand. "You must be Chase. I'm sorry, I didn't get your last name."

Chase put on his most charming smile. "I'm Chase Donaldson, and if the resort is half as good as Josephine said, it will suit my purposes well."

"Come into my office, and then I'll give you a tour. I didn't recognise Josephine Bromley's name when you first said it. When she stayed here, she was always known as Jo. It must have taken you a while to act on her recommendation."

Chase's brow creased in confusion. "Why must it be a while? From the way she spoke, I assumed she was still here. I'd love to catch up with her after the tour."

Julie gritted her teeth; she found it difficult to stay civil. The man before her, exuding charm and goodwill, had crushed Jo's self-confidence and threatened payback.

"Well, I can do the tour, but I can't help with seeing Jo. She only stayed for a few days. I'm not sure when she spoke to you about the retreat, but I'm surprised she recommended it, considering her short stay. I thought the exercise and diet regimen were too tough for her."

Chase followed Julie on the facility tour and stopped to chat with guests exercising. Julie noticed that whenever Chase stopped to talk to others, he brought up Jo's name. All the residents stuck to the plan, denying any knowledge of Josephine as he continued to call her.

The frustration was evident on Chase's face, and his body language conveyed growing anger. When he could delay no longer, Chase asked for a tour of the grounds. Julie smiled. The sneak was trying to locate Jo's car. The walk around the estate showcased the pool and the outside cabana. Chase said as they walked past the parked cars, "Are there any undercover areas for the cars?"

Julie looked at the carport roof and rolled her eyes at Chase. He noticed her reaction and followed up with,

"I can see that the roof protects the cars here, but you have a garage. Do you house cars there?"

"Mr Donaldson, the garage is my private property. My cars are in there. The carport is sufficient to accommodate the guests' cars. Now, are we finished?"

Chase nodded. "Thanks for your time. Despite Josephine's recommendations, I don't believe I'll use your retreat. Thank you all the same."

"Mr Donaldson, don't treat me like a fool. At no time did I imagine you were here for any reason other than to find this Josephine."

Chase's charming façade slipped; in its place was a sneer. Angry eyes glittered at her, and he stalked away, giving her a deadly stare. Julie felt the man's hostility hit her full force. In one respect, she felt happy that she had hidden Jo from this dangerous man, but she hoped it wouldn't come back to haunt her. The resort was all she owned, and the thought that she might have jeopardised it made her feel ill.

THIRD TIME'S THE CHARM

Now that Chase had found her, Jo decided it might be time to leave the retreat. She and Julie agreed that it was best for Jo to move on for the safety of the visitors. Jo felt as if she were leaving one of her only friends when she left the resort. Julie had been faithful to her word, and Jo was now many kilos lighter. She set out on her next adventure with a maintenance program packed in her bag.

Chapter Thirteen

J o spent her first night away from the resort in a motel, three hours away. After Chase tracked her to the health resort, Jo decided she needed to be a little shrewder with her travel plans. The first change she needed to make was disposing of her car. The car was a classic and easily recognisable. If Chase had people looking for her, she didn't want to give away her location, in case someone remembered the case.

Settled at a quaint coffee shop table, Jo decided she needed a plan. While driving and stopping on a whim was okay, she probably needed a to-do list to continue losing weight and finding a place to settle. Jo decided that the first place to start was a car dealership; from there, she would choose what else she needed to do.

After arriving at the nearest car dealership, Jo informed the agent of her preferences.

"I want an SUV, but not one so big that I need a truck licence to drive it. I don't want to be the person who takes ten minutes to turn the car around; something compact is what I want."

The sales agent showed Jo the SUVs on display in the showroom, and she chose a nifty blue SUV that should handle the terrain better than her car.

"Are you trading something ?"

She tossed her head, saying, "Yes, that's my beamer sitting in the parking lot."

The sales attendant looked in the direction Jo pointed and came to a dead stop. His mouth had fallen open, and his eyes gawked at her.

"You mean to tell me you're trading in that classic BMW for a small SUV?"

His voice rose an octave as he asked the questions, his attention fixed on the BMW.

"Only if you give me a good price for the car. We need to discuss this. Do you have an office?"

Jo had another request for the sales agent when the paperwork was complete.

"I know you probably don't want to know this, but I sold the beemer because it is too distinctive, and I'm fleeing from my husband. I can't stop you from advertising the beemer, but if someone asks about what I'm driving now, I'd appreciate it if you didn't give anyone else the make, model or rego of my new vehicle."

The sales agent said, "Ah, I wondered why you would trade a classic BMW for a regular SUV. I'll ensure that the information regarding your new purchase is safe and instruct the other salesman to keep it confidential."

Later that day, when she returned to the motel, Jo recalled how productive the day had been. Her new car wouldn't be ready until the next day, so she had some time to fill. It would be wise to check on her business managers, contact her solicitor, and speak with her sister. Jo's next challenge was finding a way to prepare meals. She needed a blender and a supply of fruit and vegetables, but how would she make that happen? A fridge to keep fresh produce in was not a challenge, but how would she run a blender and cook simple meals without a cooktop or power? Jo saw an ad for a camping goods shop as she flicked through the directory. Bingo! Tomorrow, she would visit the store to see if they could help.

She stilled her hands after pulling the band in her ponytail tight again. Moving to the mirror, she scrutinised her face. A woman approaching her thirties needed a hairstyle that was better than a relic from her teenage years. A short bob might suit her, she thought. Once again, going through the motel directory, she found a hairdresser who worked after hours on Thursday night. As she entered the unfamiliar shop, the butterflies in her stomach took flight. Was it the right thing to do? She gritted her teeth and made her way to the front counter. A young woman with purple hair operated the desk. Jo balked and stammered.

"I have an appointment, but I don't think you will suit me. Sorry."

As she turned towards the door, the young woman laughed. "The colour is a charity fundraiser. I promise I won't turn your hair purple. Why don't you take a seat, and we can discuss what you want?"

The comment reassured Jo, and she sat as the hairdresser suggested.

Before heading off the next day, Jo contacted Barry to find out how Chase had located the retreat. When Barry's receptionist answered, Jo identified herself and asked to speak with Barry.

"Jo, how goes it?" Barry greeted her.

"Things are great, and I'm ready to move on. I have a problem, which must have come from your end."

"What was the problem, and why must it come from my end?"

"Chase came to the health retreat looking for me. The other guests and the proprietor said I wasn't there, so I hid in my room. Chase got aggressive when he realised that what the others were telling him about me leaving must have been true. Julie didn't say where I was, so he gave her the uncharming side of Chase Donaldson."

"I swear I told no one about your whereabouts. Most of the time, I do not know where you are."

Jo ran her hands through her short bob and grinned despite herself. "Well, I don't know how he found out where I was staying. I've changed my vehicle and phone, so if you have a pen, I'll give you the details now. For God's sake, keep them under lock and key. I'm moving again, so it will be a day or two before I talk to you."

Once she collected her car, Jo detoured past the camping shop. The previous day, the proprietor had suggested a generator and a jug to run her blender. With that equipment, she would be self-sufficient and could continue her healthy eating programme wherever she travelled.

Excitement bubbled in her stomach as she shifted gears in her new vehicle. She had completed everything on her list. Her blond bob swung around her jaw, and the sound of the gas refrigerator hummed away in the back of her new vehicle. 'I need music to help celebrate my new life,' she told herself. After pulling to the side of the road, Jo hunted through the glove box for a particular CD. She knew it was old hat to listen to Abba, but the music was upbeat, and the songs were old favourites.

Jo's life settled into a comfortable routine. Each morning, she rose early and went for a run. On returning to her motel, she used her new blender to mix breakfast and lunch drinks. With the new refrigerator, she could keep the lunchtime drink cold, and the fruit for the next day stayed fresh in the chilling compartment. After breakfast, Jo exercised for thirty minutes, showered, and headed off to another town. Although she had been travelling for months, she still hadn't found the right place to settle. It was hard to find the proper town when you didn't know what you were looking for, but Jo thought she would know the right place when she saw it.

The light was fading, and Jo decided to stop at the next town, five kilometres away, according to her GPS. Despite the diminishing light, the distant mountain ranges were still visible. As she crested a rise, a settlement lay spread out before her. The town was tucked into the lee of the closest mountain range, and a vast expanse of water dissected the landmass. Excitement buzzed through her veins as the outskirts of the town enveloped her.

Jo took her time, driving through the deserted streets of the village. The main street had many establishments ranging from a stock feed place to a ladies' hairdresser. The shopkeepers maintained their premises well, giving them an old-world look, as though they had remained unchanged for generations. She saw a small shop lit up as she considered staying at a motel or a bed-and-breakfast. A drive past assured her that the shop was open and the establishment served food. As if on cue, her stomach rumbled. After dropping a U-turn, she pulled into a car park in front of the shop. Jo sat in the car, gazing out the window at the restaurant. The warm glow of light spilled out into the night, and inside, patrons sat at tables and in booths, talking and smiling at one another. Had she found her perfect place?

As she opened the door to the café, the loud sound of an old-fashioned bell alerted the other customers to her arrival. All eyes focused on her, and she felt self-conscious. Should she turn around and walk out?

"Hello there! Welcome to Mountain View. I'm Lindsay, and I own this eatery. Can we feed you tonight?"

The tension in her throat relaxed, and she smiled at the friendly owner. "Yes, you can feed me. I hoped it wasn't too late to find something open."

Once she placed her order, Lindsay introduced her to some other diners and took her place at the table of an older couple who invited her to join them. Conversation in the room resumed, and Jo sipped her mug of tea when the bell over the door rang again. Everyone looked up at the newcomer, and Jo's stomach lurched when she saw him. The man had his long, black hair tied at the nape of his neck and a dark beard. His form-fitting shirt and snug jeans displayed broad shoulders and a fine physique. An aggressive look in his brown eyes and the glare on his handsome face added to his air of danger.

"Do you own that blue SUV out front?" the newcomer demanded.

"Ah, yes, I do. "

"You're parking in my spot."

Jo glanced towards the window and shrugged.

"Sorry, I didn't see the reserved sign. You'd better put a larger sign up so that other tourists don't park there."

He placed his hands on his hips and said, "Well?"

Jo held her palms up and shrugged. "Well, what?"

"You need to move your car, that's what."

The noise in the room diminished when the newcomer entered, but resumed while Jo and the man spoke. Jo laughed.

"It is pointless for me to move my car so you can park there. You must have parked within walking distance, as there were few vehicles in front. Why don't we chalk it up to experience, and I'll ensure I don't park there next time?"

"No, move the damn car now and don't hurry back."

Jo looked around the room. The other customers avoided making eye contact with her. So that's how it was. My dream town turned out to be a fantasy. Jo threw money on the table and walked towards the door.

"Where is the nearest motel or B&B?"

"Two hours away."

The couple Jo had sat with shook their heads, but she kept walking. Once inside her car, she reversed out and drove away. Cruising through the back streets, she looked for somewhere secluded where she could sleep for the night. A motel or B&B two hours away was too far for her to contemplate. Jo didn't enjoy driving at night and wouldn't risk driving on unknown roads.

The moon shone through a cluster of trees, and the night air held a whisper of wind. An old shed stood at the end of a cul-de-sac, and Jo slowed to inspect it. One side of the shed faced the road, but the other was enclosed, offering an excellent place to park for the night. Resigned to eating fruit for dinner, she mourned the loss of the cooked vegetables and chicken she had ordered at the café.

Once Jo had eaten, she pulled out her sleeping bag and pillow and covered the windows with towels. Enclosed in the car, she settled for the night. Stretched out on her back seat, feeling all snug and warm in her sleeping bag, Jo thought of the bloke in the café. What rational person reacted as he did? Talk about overkill! How the other patrons had distanced themselves from the discussion was almost as bad as the man's attack. Nobody came to her defence or told the angry man he was being ridiculous. Jo had to admit that it disappointed her that this town was not where she wanted to settle, but what the hell? She had been travelling for three months, and if she had to continue, she would.

A thumping noise dragged Jo from a heavy sleep. She pulled the pillow over her ears and huddled into the sleeping bag. The car shivered and rocked from side to side. What had just happened? A male voice yelled, "Wake up, Jo."

She shimmied out of the sleeping bag with a deep groan and yanked off the towel covering the nearest window. The man from the café last night was standing next to the vehicle. Jo unlocked the door and shoved it open. As she stepped out, she said, "What now? Don't tell me! Is the shed your place? No? Is it your piece of grass, or do you take all the ladies' parking here?"

"I wanted to…"

"To move me on, I'm sure. This town is the unfriendliest place I have visited in the last three months of travelling."

"If you shut up for a moment…."

"If I stop talking, you will add more complaints about my behaviour. I don't…"

Jo's rant ended as the man grabbed her by the elbows and dragged her closer. He silenced her by placing his lips on hers, and she stilled, shock making her powerless to resist. His warm lips moved over hers, and she wasn't sure what to do. When his tongue touched her bottom lip, she groaned and opened her mouth. As he explored her mouth, Jo's heart swelled.

The kiss made her light-headed, and her skin tingled. When the stranger's hands reached out to cup her bottom, she thought she might faint. She gave in to temptation and ran her shaking hands up the cotton shirt that covered the vast expanse of his chest. As he massaged her butt cheeks, she ran her fingers through his hair. It surprised Jo how long it was; the black locks were soft and silky in her fingers.

Jo was suddenly adrift. The man had moved away, and as she opened her eyes, she noticed that his breath came in puffs. With her breathing erratic, she wondered what would happen next. This man's assault should outrage her, but the tingling along her spine and the blush spreading over her face blotted out any sense of affront.

"God, what just happened? I wanted you to stop talking. I'm sorry, I got carried away."

Jo chewed on her bottom lip. What should she do? Should she propose a truce, or should she tear strips off him for assaulting her?

"We should start anew. You know me, but I'm disadvantaged because I don't know who you are."

The man shoved out his hand. "I'm Marc Hamilton. This town is friendly, but I was rude last night, at least that's what the folk in the café said. Yesterday was a rough day, and I took it out on you. You had to sleep in your car, and that was my fault. Last night, I came to look for you, but your hiding place was pretty good. I looked this morning on the off chance you might still be in town. This town has both a motel and a B&B."

Jo wasn't sure what to do with the information about the accommodation. Did Marc think she would forgive him, and they would forget what had happened last night? His apology had seemed genuine, and the knowledge that his behaviour had outraged the café's customers warmed her heart. Was this the town she sought, even after the rocky start?

"Why don't you pack up here, and I will treat you to breakfast? It's the least I can do, seeing as I'm the reason you had no dinner last night."

Jo considered Marc's offer. If she wanted to live here, perhaps she would have to make some compromises. "I'll meet you at the café in fifteen minutes if that suits you. I'll be sure not to park in your spot."

Marc grinned and nodded. "See you soon."

When she walked into the café, the proprietor, Lindsay, greeted her.

"Hey, Jo. Glad to see our local welcoming committee didn't chase you away."

Lindsay glared at Marc, and he held his palms up in surrender.

Jo laughed. "I think we've come up with a truce. We are having breakfast together to seal the deal and to make a point; I should have one of everything on the menu."

Marc shot her an amused look. "I'll pay the bill, but I doubt a skinny little thing like you could eat her way through the menu's contents."

Skinny, was Marc describing her? She flushed with the pleasure of the compliment and grabbed the menu to survey the options. Jo needed something to look at rather than the man who had kissed her that morning. Now she knew how soft his lips were and how that tongue felt investigating her mouth, and the memory of his hand squeezing her butt caused desire to roll through her. Jo clenched her thighs together to stop the strange sensations from overwhelming her.

Lindsay served the food, and Jo's stomach rumbled at the aroma of the grilled fish and vegetables. The big jug of water she had ordered sat on the table near the condiments, and Marc stared at her meal in amazement.

"Who eats fish for breakfast? And what's the go with the vegetables and the jug of water? Are you a health freak or something?"

Jo's face flushed as she poured herself a glass of water.

"I'm not a health freak, but I try to eat well. Look at your meal. Who loads up with carbs and fat at breakfast time?"

"Whoa!" Lindsay said. "The truce is going smoothly, I see. Why don't you try for a polite conversation, Marc?"

Marc was now busy shovelling food into his mouth. Jo shook her head in amazement. Did this man have no social skills? When she finished her glass of water, she grinned at Lindsay. "Ah, has no one house-trained him yet?"

Lindsay let out a loud hoot. "Can we encourage you to stay in our little town? Marc might have met his match."

"If I stay, I can't live forever in a motel or B&B, which this town has despite my earlier beliefs. Are there any houses or flats to rent?"

Lindsay looked at Marc. The abrupt end to the conversation alerted Marc, and he looked up from his mostly empty plate.

"What did I miss?"

Jo gave him a wry glance. "Four chips and a piece of the egg."

"That's hilarious. What were you discussing that required me to pay close attention? Was I just roped into something?"

"We were discussing Jo looking for something to rent so she can stay," Lindsay said.

"Oh! We don't have many places for rent in town, but I have a house that might be suitable for you. It's outside the village, though. If you want to live in town, an empty shop might suit you."

Chapter Fifteen

Jo's face lit up when she spied Marc's house through the trees. An old Queenslander, the house stood on an acre of cleared land, surrounded by dense bush. Although the gardens needed attention, the old house was in good repair. The house, constructed in a traditional style, was accessed by steps leading up to the main door. There was a space for her car underneath the house, and the laundry facilities were located downstairs.

When Jo walked through the dwelling, she could tell that some areas of the house had undergone extensive renovations in the past. The updates were practical without spoiling the original features of the house. Fretwork over the doors remained, as did the tongue-and-groove construction on the walls. The bedroom floors were plushly carpeted, but the flooring in the other rooms was polished, featuring traditional floorboards enhanced by throw rugs.

Marc watched Jo as she explored his house. Her joy in simple things intrigued him, and watching her laugh drew his focus back to her kissable lips. She affected him in ways he hadn't experienced in years, making him uncomfortable. He wasn't getting involved with any woman, and certainly not with one who might up and leave on a whim.

"Marc, this house is just perfect! How come you own a lovely house and don't live in it?"

Despite his reservations, Marc smiled. "I don't live in it because I own property just out of town. The house was my grandparents' house, so I don't want to sell it, but the town doesn't have much call for rentals. Do you have any furniture?"

"Yeah, but I'd sooner find pieces that fit the house's era. Are there any second-hand shops or antique places?"

"You'll have to go to Lakeside, an hour away. Two shops sell furniture, and there's a cabinet maker, although he might be expensive."

"This is exciting! I must stay at the B&B for another week or two while I get this set up, but I'm eager to start. Can we fill out the paperwork straight away? Thank you, Marc, for letting me rent your house."

In her excitement, Jo hugged Marc. His arms slid around her, and the friendly embrace turned into something more. Her pulse raced as Marc tilted her head and covered her lips with his. With a gasp of dismay, he dropped his hands and stepped back as though her touch had burned him. Dazed and bemused, Jo stood immobile.

"God, I did it again! What is it that makes me assault you when we get close? Can we forget this?"

Jo chuckled. "Hell, no! I've never had that reaction from any man. I intend to savour the moments when you lose control."

"Are you fishing for compliments? You are telling me guys aren't lining up to take you out??"

"I'll tell you the story one day, but I'm not fishing for compliments. Men have never been interested in me."

Marc shook his head, bemused at the turn of this conversation.

"I brought the paperwork with me on the off chance you liked the house. Give me a minute while I grab it from the car, and then we can sign them on that bench."

While Jo waited for Marc to return, she continued to walk through the house. She intended to return later with a pen and paper to list the furniture and fittings she thought were necessary. The items that Jo had removed from her townhome were unsuitable for this place and would be a reminder of the life she had left behind. She needed no reminders of her humiliation or her depressive eating habits. This town gave her a new start, and she intended to seize it with both hands.

Marc walked back into the house, his head down, sorting through the stack of papers in his hand. His good looks struck Jo once again. There was a physical attraction, but might there be more? Her husband's presence or chaste kisses never warmed her heart and made her body tremble with desire. Maybe if Chase heated her blood and made her mind go blank, the intimacies she shared with her husband might have been pleasurable. Marc caught Jo staring at him. With a warning shake of his head, he skirted around her to lay the paperwork on the bench. Once he handed her a pen, he stepped quickly away. Keeping his distance seemed the best idea; he couldn't get drawn into her web if he kept her at a distance.

Later that night, as Jo snuggled in bed, she gripped her mobile phone. Her fingers tapped on the covers as she waited for her solicitor, Barry, to pick up the phone. She had resigned herself to leaving a message when an abrupt "Hello" was on the other end of the line. Jo grinned to herself; he was always abrupt on the phone. "Good evening, Barry!"

"Jo! I was worried about you. Where are you, and why haven't you been in touch with me? Didn't we agree on a check-in once a week?"

"We did, and I'm sorry, but I've been busy. I've rented a house, and I need furniture for it. A small town in the mountains is to be my new home. That's one reason I've called you."

"So you want me to organise to send your furniture to that little town in the back of Burke?"

"The place is called Mountain View and is an hour away from a regional town called Lakeside."

"Are you still in New South Wales?"

"No, I crossed into Queensland five hundred kilometres ago. The district is stunning, and the townsfolk are friendly. Anyhow, about my furniture. Don't send it; please sell it. I don't care how much you get for it or even if you donate it to a charity. My new home is an old Queenslander, and I intend to buy furniture that fits the house's period. That furniture holds only horrid memories, and I want a fresh start."

There was silence on the phone, and Jo wondered if she had lost the connection.

"Okay, I can do that. I'm just making notes to remind myself what you need," Barry said. Jo had set up a mailbox at the post office after Marc had explained that the postie didn't deliver out of town, so she relayed her postal address to Barry.

"Is that all?"

"Hm, yeah, that's it for now. I have an internet connection, so I can still conduct reviews with my management team. If you keep a close eye on things, all should be well. Everything is going well, but I'm wondering if I should set up those meetings to be fortnightly or even weekly?"

"Ah, weekly might take the management team away from their daily tasks too often. Taking more interest in the business might wake up a few unenthusiastic admins, and a meeting once a fortnight should often be enough."

Barry cleared his throat, and Jo knew this was a precursor to the unpleasant news.

"There is good news and bad news, as the joke goes. What do you want first?"

"Give me the good news first, please."

"Well, the good news is that we've sold the house, and I disbursed the money as you asked. You got the asking price for it. Consistent with your instructions to the real estate agent, the sale went through quickly after she restricted viewing to those who could prove their ability to buy the property."

"Okay, that's great, Barry. Hit me with the bad news."

"Well, the bad news is that Chase refuses to sign the papers even though you filed for divorce three months ago. He is holding out for alimony payments, and although I explained to his solicitor that you wouldn't pay alimony, his lawyer says otherwise."

"Did you use your investigator's photos of him with Kelly?"

"Yes, but he says he needed physical relief as you refused your marital duties."

"Ha! marital duties, my foot! You need to be in the same place to participate in intimacy, and Chase was never home. I paid off his car and left him with $10,000 in our joint account. Doesn't that count as payment?"

"No, he wants ten thousand dollars a month."

"With most of my money tucked away in the Cayman Islands and the businesses held in a company name, he shouldn't be able to prove I have enough money to scratch myself with, should he?"

"No, he shouldn't, but he isn't giving up."

"How tiresome! Remind me next time I want to get married; we need a prenuptial agreement. That would save all this hassle. Hold out with the no alimony, and we'll see how long he waits."

"You need a prenuptial agreement, do you? Have you met Mr Right already?"

"God, no! What if you organised a once-off payment for Chase? Could you wrap up a legal agreement that pays him once, but he can't return for more later ?"

"Yeah, the problem is that I don't know how much he'd want. He appears to know you're wealthy, and he won't settle for a pittance. You might get rid of him for a million dollars, but do you want to go there?"

"Hell, no! The bastard only married me for my money, so let him stew. I can wait him out."

After Barry hung up, Jo lay in bed and contemplated the problem of Chase. How could she extricate herself from a drawn-out battle over money? Was there a way to get Chase to encourage him to leave her alone? Perhaps she needed to speak with the investigator who had taken the photos of Chase and Kelly and ask him to follow Chase to see if anything untoward was happening. Further investigation might yield something useful. Jo resolved to suggest this to Barry the next time they talked.

Chapter Sixteen

Jo spent the following days hunting for furniture in the shops in Lakeside; she hardly ventured into town. Some pieces of furniture she found needed repair, while others looked as good as new. Although not skilled in woodwork, she knew she could do minor repairs, but other parts required professional restoration.

She purchased linens and crockery in a whirl of activity and replaced the cutlery and cooking utensils she had disposed of when she sold her house. As a rule, Jo didn't enjoy shopping. Whenever she went into a shop, she felt self-conscious about her size, and the shop assistants always tried to hurry her through her purchases. Her recent experience with Pam made her braver, but shopping in Lakeside was a whole new ball game. It was easier to shop for bedding and linen because there was no 'acceptable' size for towels or sheets so that she could browse and buy to her heart's content.

With parcels and boxes surrounding her, she didn't hear the car pull up in the driveway. When someone knocked on the door, she jumped at the sudden sound. Lindsay stood at the door, and Jo was surprised to see her.

"Hi, Lindsay. What a pleasant surprise!"

"Hi, yourself! We haven't seen you around town, and I thought I'd pop out to ensure you were all right."

Jo opened the door wider. "Come in. I'll show you what has kept me occupied."

Jo led Lindsay into the lounge room, and Lindsay smiled at the profusion of boxes and packages strewn over the floor.

"My God, woman, you sure know how to shop!"

"I haven't had as much fun ever as buying things for this place. I love the house, and I want to do it well. Some furniture needs touch-ups, and some pieces that need serious refurbishment are still in

Lakeside with the restorers. Once it's all done, the house should look fabulous."

Lindsay pointed at the parcels. "Will you show me what you bought?"

Lindsay and Jo pulled out bedding, towels, and crockery for the next half hour. As Lindsay exclaimed over the things she had purchased, Jo hoped she had made a friend for the first time.

The women sat in the kitchen, propped on stools at the bench. The dining setting that Jo found needed restoration, and the restorer had promised to replace the ruined chairs with authentic-looking pieces. Lindsay relayed the local gossip, and then the talk moved to their backgrounds and where Jo had originated. Jo was wary but confided that she was trying to put a failed marriage behind her. Lindsay was astute enough to realise that a mystery surrounded her. When she changed the conversation, Lindsay happily complied.

Jo waved her off from the front door two hours after Lindsay arrived. A smile spread across her face. Her decision to stop in the town for a meal was one of the best decisions on her voyage across the country. She knew she would see more of Lindsay in the immediate future because Lindsay had asked her to join the local book club. When she hesitated, Lindsay laughed and said that sometimes they didn't get to read the proposed book, and that the ladies just got together to chat.

Jo ventured into town to the book club two days later, and her nerves jiggled around in her stomach. She had never been invited to a book club meeting before. The women in the book club took turns hosting the sessions, with each hostess providing a plate of food and the wine.

As a new member, Jo hadn't read the book. The ladies took that as an excuse to put the book review on hold. The members' ages ranged from 23 to 35, and all were articulate and friendly. Jo revelled in the experience. One lady, Caroline, lamented her inability to find a nanny.

Small communities without employment didn't attract backpackers or younger visitors.

While the women chatted, Jo gave thought to Caroline's plight. Caroline enjoyed being at home, but worked for a fledgling company that might eventually hire four or five other townspeople. A business that generated jobs was worth pursuing, but she needed to take her children with her, which would have hindered its viability. Caroline's husband, Noah, did more than his fair share of minding and cut his business hours to accommodate his wife's new venture, but they needed a nanny to take the pressure off the parents.

When the evening drew to a close, Jo mulled over Caroline's problem. She didn't need to work, but if she remained at home without earning an income, people would question her source of support. Could Jo look after the kids? She didn't even know the children's ages. Would Caroline trust her to watch over her children? Did she want a full-time job? The questions rolled around in Jo's head even after she had retired for the night.

Jo ventured into town, hoping to locate Caroline. A slow drive through the main street didn't turn up any new-looking businesses. Where to now? She explored some side roads. If she still hadn't found Caroline, she intended to stop at the café and ask Lindsay for directions.

Just as Jo was ready to concede defeat, she noticed an old building with fresh paintwork and a new awning at the front. The renewed building looked promising. When she read the name of the shop, she burst out laughing. The business's name was New Beginnings, and it appeared to Jo that this was fate. After parking the car, she walked toward the shop. She didn't know what Caroline sold, and the store's exterior did nothing to remove that doubt. When she pushed the door open, screaming assailed Jo's senses. There were no other sounds, and the hairs rose on her neck. What could make a child cry like that? Jo hurried towards the sound and then pushed open the door. The scene that unfolded before her evoked sympathy within her. A child of three or four was flat out on the floor, shrieking. A smaller child sat sobbing, and Caroline stood in a corner with tears running down her face. Shock immobilised Jo for a minute, and then her senses kicked in.

She glared at the hysterical child and shouted, "Stop!" Two pairs of identical brown eyes shot up to look at her. The little girl's hiccupping sobs broke the silence that ensued. Caroline ran her shaking fingers through her hair as her face flushed bright red.

"Bad day?" Jo asked.

Caroline groaned. "Bad year. We met yesterday, didn't we?" Caroline said, moving forward as she brushed her dress and straightened her hair.

"Thanks for the intervention."

Jo lifted the little girl, who was still sobbing on the floor. "Sh, sweetie, it's okay. The noise has stopped."

The little girl hid her face in Jo's shoulder, and Jo gently patted her on the back.

"Why don't I put the kettle on, and you can tell me why you're here? Unless you have a significant party for me to organise?"

"No party, but a proposition we might discuss."

As Caroline began preparing the tea, the little boy fussed.

"I don't want to be here. I want to go to the park." He stamped his foot and raised his voice. Caroline looked flustered but did nothing to stop the child from whining. She sent a beseeching glance at Jo as the crescendo of the boy's demands grew.

"Do you want me to handle this? I'm not as emotionally involved as you."

"Please, be my guest. I'm all out of patience today, as you saw."

Jo put the little girl down and squatted beside the boy, whose whining had reached massive proportions.

"Stop that noise. You have made your mummy and little sister sad. Only kids who can behave themselves get to go to the park, and you are not behaving right now. Sit on the mat and play with your sister while I chat with your mummy."

The small boy, Tyler, gaped at Jo and sat on the floor with his sister. Caroline sighed in relief and entered the tiny kitchenette to prepare morning tea. Once they all had food, Caroline said, "So, to what do I owe the pleasure?"

Jo hesitated for a moment. "This is presumptuous of me, but I need a job. Yesterday, you told me you were looking for a nanny, and although I have no formal training, I thought my problem could be your solution."

Caroline gazed at Jo. Jo held her hand in surrender as a red flush rushed to her neck and cheeks.

"It's fine; you don't have to say anything. It was just a thought."

"No, no! It's a great idea. I'm just stunned. How do you envisage this working?"

"Um, I hadn't given it much thought. I'm not sure what you have in mind for my duties other than looking after the children. Could we start with a day or two to see how it goes? You'll want to do a police check, and I can give you my details."

"I need to talk to Noah, my husband, about this, but he'll be in favour as the child-minding thing eats into his week."

Jo nodded, relief coursing through her body. "I was worried about talking to you. I wasn't sure if you would think I was overstepping the mark. So, the next question is, where is the p-a-r-k?" Jo spelled out. "If you're okay with me taking them for an hour?"

Chapter Seventeen

Jo rolled out of bed and pulled on her running gear when the alarm sounded. As she went through her warm-up routine, she contemplated the day ahead. Caroline would be ready to leave when she arrived at the house, but Noah didn't go to work until thirty minutes later. Today was a trial, and Jo expected a random visit from Noah to check how things were going. She hoped that when he visited, everything would be peaceful.

The door opened almost before she knocked. Jo was engulfed in the early morning chaos as mums and dads prepared for their day and the children demanded attention. Jo put her bag and a box on the kitchen counter and started making the kids ' breakfast. Caroline gave her a sheet of paper as she kissed her husband and children goodbye and left.

Noah was still dressing and shaving, so Jo sat at the table to supervise the kids.

"What's in the box, Jo?" asked Tyler.

"I'll show you when you finish breakfast and clean your teeth. There's a toy for you to play with and one for Maddy."

"You brought us presents?"

"No, the toys are for you to play with, but we must return them. I can borrow something else for you and Maddy when I return them. It's called a toy library."

After kissing his children goodbye, Noah left minutes later. Jo experienced a moment of panic; she was now responsible for these two children. What was she thinking? Jo did not know what a nanny did. She grabbed the sheet of paper Caroline had left for her and read the dot points. Okay, that looked easy enough, and if it wasn't on the list, she could improvise.

At morning tea, Jo settled Maddy in her high chair with a bowl of blackberries, while Tyler sat at the table with a Vegemite sandwich. Noah made an unscheduled visit that Jo had expected. She felt reassured that nothing was happening and that Noah could leave without worrying, but to her surprise, he made himself a drink and sat down with his children.

"It's okay for you to eat and drink, too," he said with a grin.

"I don't eat morning tea, and I'll organise my lunch when Maddy sleeps, and Tyler has TV time."

Noah shrugged. "Whatever suits you."

Jo cleaned the kids up after morning tea and found hats and sunscreen. Caroline left the washing to hang out, which was a good time for the kids to have outside time. As she hung the washing out, she laughed at how quickly her life had changed. Nobody here knew that she was a fat person in disguise, and with increased self-assurance, she interacted with new people. This job was so far out of her comfort zone that it had taken a massive leap of faith to offer to help Caroline.

With Maddy in bed and Tyler nestled in front of the television, Jo took a moment to relax. A hunt through Caroline's cupboards had yielded a food processor, and she made a smoothie using the fruit in the fridge. She had finished drinking her lunchtime fare when Tyler entered the room.

"What's wrong, mate?"

The television is showing the news. I don't want to watch that."

Jo rose from her chair. "Let's see."

The television showed the breaking news. The program was not on; they had made way for a report on the latest terrorist attack in Europe. Sympathy for the victims washed over her, but her job was to protect Tyler from viewing the news footage. She led him back into the kitchen and racked her brain for something to replace the time he had spent watching television.

"Do you want to cook?" she asked the little boy.

"Yeah, grandma sometimes cooks things and lets me help."

When Noah called in later, he found the bench covered with iced patty cakes and muffins. Even though Tyler randomly applied icing to some cakes, the cupcakes still looked tasty.

"Daddy, Daddy, look what Jo and I made!"

Noah tousled the little boy's hair and said, "And what did Maddy make?"

Jo and Tyler looked at each other and laughed. "A mess, Daddy. She made a mess. Jo had to bathe her before we ate."

Noah laughed and shook his head. He kissed the toddler's head and grabbed a muffin before leaving.

Later, when Caroline opened the door, the smell that wafted out to greet her made her mouth water. She found her children on the couch, on either side of Jo, with a large book spread out before them. The scene looked so peaceful that tears welled up in Caroline's eyes. Who was this angel who had dropped into their lives? Caroline silently thanked whoever had made Jo look for a new place to settle.

Caroline asked Jo to work the whole week because the trial period had gone off without a hitch. Jo now holds her weekly business meetings using Skype on Fridays.

"I need a day off, as I have business interests to oversee. The sessions are on Friday, but I can change the day to another if you'd prefer."

Caroline nodded. "My busiest day is Friday; I'll have to work from home if you aren't available. What if I close the shop on Mondays, and you could have your day off if that works?"

With the business meetings rearranged, Jo spent the remaining four days of the week with the kids. She discovered that the children had hectic lives. Caroline had enrolled the kids in a playgroup where a group of mothers got together to allow the children to socialise. Each mother took turns organising activities, and the women supervised the kids while gossiping and drinking tea or coffee. For the first week, Jo felt awkward. While she was a woman in charge of children, she wasn't a mother and couldn't discuss the same things mothers did.

The following week, her salvation came in the form of a man. A man walked into the gathering, holding the hand of a small girl and cradling a baby in his arms. He flushed before speaking.

"Hi, I'm James, and these are my children, Bethany and Amy. As the stay-at-home dad in my family, I thought it would be a good idea to join your group if you're comfortable with my presence." Jo watched the other women weigh up the odds.

When the silence stretched out awkwardly, she made the decision no one else appeared willing to make.

"Welcome, James. I am sure that being male won't be a problem for you. I'm a nanny, not a mum, and the ladies have welcomed me into their group. The group is a playgroup, so it's all about children. Without dads, these ladies wouldn't be mums," she laughed.

After James' acceptance into the group, Jo gravitated towards him at most of the sessions. He was uncomfortable with the child-related conversations that the other mothers had, so she chatted with James about world and community events.

When Jo arrived at the children's swimming lessons on Friday, it was a lovely surprise to find James at the pool. There was a half-hour break between the kids' lessons, so Jo needed to dress Tyler, set him up with snacks and activities, and then get into the water with Maddy. James' eldest daughter was in the same group as Tyler, and the baby was in Maddy's set. The more she saw of James, the more she liked him. He was an amusing and intelligent conversationalist, and his manner with his girls was loving and affectionate. Despite his bookish air, he had a wicked sense of humour. James's round glasses framed sharp blue eyes, and his brown, wavy hair looked like it was winning the war. Jo had no attraction to James and was glad he tackled the awkward conversation one day at the pool.

" I'm about to start a conversation, and it is embarrassing, but it needs to be said. I like you and love talking to and arguing with you, but I hope you aren't reading something romantic into our times together."

Jo smiled. "James, you are my ideal man as a brother or best friend. I have no romantic attachments to you and enjoy our time together. Is spending time with you a problem?"

James grinned. "Us spending time together is not an issue. My wife, Rachel, said I might have given you the wrong idea. I didn't think so, but it's best to clear the air."

One morning, when Tyler was unusually irritable, Jo decided to visit the park. Just as she strapped Maddy into her car seat, her phone rang.

"Hey, Jo. It's James. Have you noticed what a nice day today is?"

She laughed. "Did you call to give me a weather report?"

She heard him chuckle on the other end of the phone. "No, can I convince you to come to the park with us? Bethany is cranky, and I thought outside time and some company other than her little sister and me might make her happier."

"I have a stroppy child here, too. I'm just strapping the kids into the car because we're going to the park."

"I'll meet you there."

Chapter Eighteen

Jo smiled as she looked up at the old Queenslander. No matter how many times she made this homecoming trip, a well of happiness overwhelmed her whenever she pulled up in the driveway of her home.

As she grabbed her shopping, she walked to the front door and hefted the bags onto her hip, giving her the leverage to use her keys. The glass panels of the old door shone in the sunlight as she pushed it open. She deposited the shopping and walked to the sink to fill the kettle. The tap dripped. The dripping was an annoyance; no matter how hard Jo tried to turn it off, it continued.

Jo pulled out her phone and dialled Mark's phone number as the kettle heated. She didn't expect a warm welcome; the last time she had seen him, he had all but run for the door, but as her landlord, it was his job to organise repairs.

Marc answered after the first three rings. "Hello, Marc here."

"Marc, hi, it's Jo."

There was no response, and she was sure he would hang up on her for a moment.

"Marc, are you there?"

"Ah, yeah, sure. What do you want?"

"The tap over the sink is dripping. Even though I've tried to turn it off hard, it drips. It needs a new washer. Do you want me to call a plumber?"

Marc let out a laugh. "You're not in the city now; there is no plumber to call. When do you want me to fix the tap?"

"Monday is my day off. If you want to do it, then."

"Okay, Monday it is."

Monday dawned sunny, and Jo considered calling Marc and rescheduling his visit. The temperature had warmed enough for a swim in the lake, although the water from the mountain stream would be chilly. She had found a sheltered spot on the riverbank, and the temptation to play hooky was great. She had just decided to swim when a car pulled into the driveway. "Drat," she said to herself. Oh well, might as well have the tap fixed sooner rather than later. Marc stomped up the stairs and raised his hand to knock. Jo opened the door before his fist connected with it.

"Why don't you have the chain on the door? You should check who is here before you open the door. I could have been anyone."

"When you drove into the driveway, I looked out."

He raised his hands in surrender and then walked past her and into the kitchen.

"Do you need me to help?"

"No, this job is straightforward. I'll turn the water off, so you won't be able to use it for a few minutes."

Marc walked through the kitchen and out into the backyard. The water connection must be out there. Jo tried not to watch Marc as his arms flexed and strained, but it was an arduous task. When Marc had stormed into the cafe, she thought he was sexy, but their kisses seared themselves into her brain. When Jo took a large breath, Marc looked up at her. The blood rushed to her face, and she ducked her head. Imagine being caught drooling over the landlord.

Marc collected his tools a few minutes later and walked outside to turn on the water. Jo waited in the kitchen, and when he returned, she offered to make a drink.

"Ah, no. Thanks, all the same."

She walked with him to the front door. When he turned to say goodbye, they met face to face. Jo watched as Marc's eyes closed, and his gaze lingered on her lips when he opened them. He moved closer and leaned over to place his lips on her mouth. Jo leaned against the wall for support as he nibbled her lower lip. Marc deepened the kiss, his tongue pushing for entry into her mouth.

With his body plastered against her, Marc pulled up Jo's shirt and palmed her breasts. Jo heard a moan; she was so breathless and dizzy that she wasn't sure if it was Marc or her. The pressure of his hands made her nipples peak, and she wanted to see what happened next. As the idea crossed her mind, Marc pulled away. Jo groaned. Marc's breaths came in short and rapid bursts, as did hers.

"Ah, I should be going."

Jo grabbed Marc by the arm. "You've done this three times now. Can't you keep going so I know what happens next? Damn, you twist me in knots and walk away."

Marc shook his head. "If we go any further, I won't be able to stop. Quit while you're ahead, Jo."

Grabbing the front of his shirt in her fists, she yelled,

"Are you stupid? I don't want to stop! I want to discover what happens when people are attracted to each other. Is it still embarrassing, messy and painful, or are the romance novels right, and it's an earth-shattering experience?"

The look on Marc's face made Jo cringe. Watching his face turn pale and his jaw open, Jo felt like the worst fool in the world. "Sorry, I shouldn't have put you on the spot. You'd better leave before I threaten your virtue more."

"You think what happens next is embarrassing, messy, and painful?"

The colour flooded her face, but this time she looked straight into Marc's eyes instead of trying to hide her embarrassment. "Well, my one experience was a great disappointment."

"Whoever the man was who made you embarrassed and hurt, he was a fool. God help me, this has to be a mistake, but I can't deny the challenge. Let's see what we can do to remove that memory and replace it with something nice."

Jo's pulse sped up, and her hands shook as she stepped toward Marc. She pushed his t-shirt up and ran her fingers across the muscles that hard physical work had developed. Unlike Chase's gym hours, Marc's defined muscles came from manual labour and farm work.

When he tensed and groaned as her fingers skimmed his nipples, she smiled to herself. One fist gripped her hair, and the other slid along her body. Suddenly, she was against a hot, hard body as Marc kissed her senselessly. Marc eased her back into the kitchen, and she perched on the tabletop. Jo's world tilted when he parted her legs and stepped into the space between them. He peeled off her t-shirt and palmed her breasts. As his head moved towards her peaked nipples, a banging sound became audible. Marc shot his head up and listened for a moment.

"Hello! Anyone home?" Lindsay's voice called out.

"Shit!" Mark cursed. He smoothed his shirt and dashed towards the front door. When he entered the hallway, he saw Lindsay with her head poked through the front door.

"Hi, Lindsay. Did Jo know you were calling? She had a nap, so I don't think she expected you. I can call her." Marc babbled but didn't want Lindsay to go into the kitchen if Jo was still dressing.

The door from the lounge room opened, and Jo walked out. A flush stained her cheeks, and she ran her hands through her hair as she tried to smooth it. Marc cringed. Jo was flushed, her hair was messy, and she had kiss-swollen lips. Lindsay couldn't help but miss the signs of their attempted lovemaking.

"Hi Lindsay, what a pleasant surprise. I was having a nap while Marc fixed the kitchen taps." Turning to Marc, Jo said,

"Are you finished?"

"Yeah, I'll collect my tools and leave you, ladies, to it, okay?"

Once Marc departed, Lindsay laughed. "I have never seen him flustered. I interrupted something, didn't I?"

"That obvious, was it?"

"Yeah. Marc is never verbose, and he all but babbled at me. Do you want to talk about it?"

"No, because I'm not sure we know what's happening."

"Okay, tell me if I can help. I came to see if you want to go to Lakeside for some shopping and lunch?"

"That's a splendid idea. Give me a minute to tidy up, and I'll be ready."

Chapter Nineteen

The discount store that Natalie Frost ran in Mountain View was directly across from the park. As the woman looked out the window, she pursed her lips. Tutting and shaking her head, she spoke to her shop assistant.

"Rachel is foolishly trusting. That woman and James spend an extraordinary amount of time together. They're in the park at least once a week, and Sonia said they're as thick as thieves in playgroup."

The shop assistant peered out of the window.

"They appear mighty friendly."

The old-fashioned doorbell rang as a customer entered the shop. "Hi, Natalie. Hi Alice. What's so interesting that you're looking at through the window?"

"Well, I'm not one to gossip, but have you noticed how friendly James and Jo are? I was saying Rachel is too trusting."

The newcomer peered out the window with the other two women. "Hm, we should warn Rachel about what is going on. Do you believe Caroline knows her children are dragged over the countryside while that woman meets strange men?"

"A warning mightn't go astray."

After their trip to the park, Jo and the children said goodbye to their friends and returned home. Upon arrival, they had lunch, and then it was time for Maddy to take a nap. Tyler pulled a chair over to the bench, and he and Jo made dinner. Tyler loved cooking, and she allowed him to help as much as possible.

The sound of the front door drew her attention away from the almost completed evening meal.

"Mummy!" yelled Tyler.

"Sh," Jo said. "Maddy is still asleep."

Caroline leaned over and hugged Tyler. "Hi, Ty; how's it going?"

"Jo and I have just finished making dinner. It will be yummy!"

Caroline turned questioning eyes to Jo. "Tyler helped?"

Jo nodded. "Tyler is an aspiring chef who helps me most days with dinner. He is helpful and enjoys cooking. How could I refuse his help?"

"Well, how good is that? I'll tell Dad how helpful you are, Ty. Just now, though, I need to speak to Jo alone. Let's see if we can find something on the telly."

"No, mummy. Jo bought me a puzzle, so I want to do it."

Once Tyler settled in the lounge room, Caroline put the kettle on and made cups of tea.

"Jo, I need to discuss something with you."

"Did I do something wrong with the kids? Whatever the problem is, I hope we can work it out because I enjoy spending time with them."

Caroline shook her head. "What you are doing with the kids is exceptional, and I'm grateful that you approached me for the job. The problem is the town gossip. People have seen you at the park with James. Sonia, who loves to chat, has said that you and James are as thick as thieves at playgroup. I need to ask you, is something going on between you two?"

A low groan escaped from Jo's mouth.

"Damn, I had forgotten how small-town gossip spreads. Caroline, the only thing going on between James and me is friendship. At playgroup, the other mothers discuss baby milestones, potty training, and other topics that don't interest me. As the only bloke in the group, James is self-conscious and is uninterested in baby talk. As a result, we sit together and discuss world events and other stuff."

"Okay, so no attraction happening there?"

Jo chuckled. "Have you had a good look at James? He's a cuddly nerd. Those glasses and the untamed hair don't make my girl parts sit up and take notice. He's splendid company, and Rachel prompted the friendship conversation ages ago."

"Thank goodness! I don't want to lose you. If Rachel, you, and I know about this, that's all that counts. Noah rarely listens to gossip, but I'll tell him when he returns tonight."

Jo fidgeted and then looked Caroline in the eye.

"Can I ask you something?"

"Sure."

"Well, when I arrived, I saw Marc around often. After that unforgettable introduction, I always ran into him in town. Since he rented the house to me, I have never seen him. It doesn't matter when I go to the café on a Wednesday night, Monday, Thursday, or any night. He's never there. Do you know why he's the invisible man?"

"Now that you mentioned it, you're right. I don't know why he hasn't been into town." A frown crossed Caroline's face, and her hand supported her chin.

"Do you think it would be too forward of me to visit him at home and find out what's happening?"

"Why should you be the person to see what's going on?"

Jo screwed up her face. "I need to be the person because he is avoiding me."

"Didn't you two sort out your problem?"

"We did," Jo said, "But we have an attraction between us, and I'm sure he is avoiding me."

Caroline rose from her seat and flicked the kettle back on. "Attraction? That's interesting. Marc hasn't had a relationship with a woman since discovering his fiancée and best friend in bed. A furore ensued, and the other two left town. They broke up soon after, and Jill, the fiancée, returned to town to persuade Marc to resume the relationship. It was horrid. He vowed not to trust a woman again. If he has an attraction to you, he will avoid you."

"Oh, okay. Do you think I should offer to stay away? I should give Marc the option to come into town without running into me. We could stagger the days or something?"

Caroline said, "That might work. Tell me, why are you sure Marc is attracted to you? And do you feel the same?"

Jo blushed. "He's kissed me three times; once after he found me camped in my car and once when we negotiated the lease. As well as the other day when he came to fix the taps."

"This is between you and me, okay?" asked Caroline. "Is he any good at kissing?"

Jo snorted. The less-than-ladylike sound made Caroline laugh, and Jo joined in the humour. With a shuddering breath, she said, "He is divine. He makes me go tingly, and my mind goes somewhere else, but it's obvious from his reaction he doesn't want to pursue any connection with me."

"Then it's time for you to confront him about avoiding you and organise something so you can come to town without embarrassment."

Chapter Twenty

Jo drove over the bumpy dirt road. The drive from her house to Marc's place took thirty minutes. She planned to arrive after he had stopped work for the day. Thin, twisted gum trees dotted the paddocks, and some had fire damage. With Caroline's directions and the GPS, Jo hoped to find Marc's house on the dirt roads.

She took the right-hand road at a junction and, a few minutes later, came across a letterbox with the name Hamilton printed on it. She forced herself to drive through the open gate and along the winding driveway that led to the house.

When she descended from the car, she knew why Marc did not live in the old Queenslander. The ultra-modern building gave magnificent views over the neighbouring mountain ranges. Jo ascended the stairs that led to the front door. She knocked and waited for a response.

Noise from behind her informed her of Marc's presence. He appeared to have just finished work for the day; his long hair was loose, and he wore a pair of snug jeans streaked with dirt.

"People in the country don't use the front door. You might as well come around the back while I wash."

She hadn't expected him to welcome her with open arms, but even for him, this was blunt. Jo followed him to the back door with no other choice and watched as he washed at the outdoor sink.

Once his face and hands were clean, Marc turned toward her. "What are you doing here?"

Jo shifted uneasily, her gaze fixated on the spot over his shoulder. With a shake of her head, she directed her attention back to Marc. "We need to talk."

Marc backed up so fast that she expected him to trip in his haste to move away from her. "Oh, no, you don't! I want nothing to do with you, and if you persist, I will evict you."

"I'm sorry I asked you to… ah… show me what happens when an attraction occurs between two people. It didn't appear to be a great hardship for you. Now you're acting like a thirteen-year-old virgin cornered by three horny guys. I can take no for an answer. I want to talk to you, not molest you. It's about when you go into town."

Marc glared at her. "Now you're around every corner. I won't go into town."

"I was afraid of that. You shouldn't have to stop doing the things you've done for years because of me. If we work out a day for me to eat at Lindsay's, you can go without running into me any other day."

"What day do you want to eat at the café?"

"Any day you choose, except Thursday, because I attend a book club meeting on Thursday nights."

"Okay, go on a Tuesday, and then I can go any other night. Is that it? Are we finished talking? Then you can leave."

Jo shook her head. "God, you're a rude bastard. Anyone listening would think you are so irresistible to women that they drop their knickers on the ground when they see you coming. You are the most exasperating man I have ever met. If I recall, you kissed me. If you don't want to pursue the attraction between us, that's fine. You don't need to be rude. Tell me you made a mistake, and that's that." She turned on her heel and stalked away from him. When she reached her car, she turned back towards where he had been standing; the porch was empty.

Marc watched Jo storm towards the car from the front room window. When she turned, he stepped back from the window so she didn't see him watching. He had been alone for the last three years and would not get involved with someone passing through town. But God, the woman, affected him. She was fiery and spunky, yet childlike in her naivety on other occasions. Her lips were soft and plump, and her curves fit into his palms. Her curvy body and blond hair made him want to kiss her again. He slapped his hands against his thighs and walked away from the window.

As Jo drove back towards town, she stewed over Marc's backlash. What was wrong with the guy? Even given the history Caroline had spoken of, his reaction was extreme. He had kissed her, not the other way around. She had asked him not to stop the last time, but she didn't think her request was abhorrent to him.

Her phone chirped as she pulled into the driveway, showing a message. When she flicked the screen across, her blood ran cold. The text message said, 'I have your number, soon I will have your address. Be prepared to pay up or else.'

Jo felt faint; the blood in her veins pumped so hard that the only thing she could hear was the sound of her pulse. The knots in her stomach made her nauseous. She bolted from the car to vomit and retch under a nearby tree. Wiping her mouth with the back of her hand, she staggered towards the house.

Once inside, she slammed the front door locks shut, then ran back to check that it was secure. Questions assaulted her brain. How could Chase have her number? Could he have got her address? Only Barry had the details for her new phone, and she knew, without a doubt, that he hadn't betrayed her.

With shaking fingers, she punched in the number two on her speed dial and waited for Barry to answer.

"Jo, hi. I didn't expect a call from you for another few days. What can I do for you?"

At the sound of the friendly voice, Jo lost her control and sobbed as she tried to tell Barry what had happened.

"Jo, take a deep breath and start again. I don't know what you're telling me."

Her breath hitched as she tried to gain control. "I received a text message from Chase. He threatened me and told me to pay up or else. How did he get my number? Who did you give it to, Barry? Damn, I'm so scared."

Barry supplied a four-letter expletive as his first response.

"You know me better than to think I would share your information with anyone else."

"Well, someone is accessing your files and supplying Chase with information. The health resort was not a fluke, and now the phone number. Find out where your leak is before he presents himself at my front door, for God's sake. Take my files home; there can't be a leak then."

"Send me a copy of your text, and I'll see if I can get a restraining order because of the threat in the message."

Jo spent a sleepless night testing locks and jumping at the bushland noises that, a few days ago, had sounded peaceful. When the alarm went off, she didn't go for a run in case Chase was hiding somewhere. Today was a workday, and while Jo didn't think Chase could find her at Caroline's home, she worried about leaving her home vacant for the day. Could Chase get into the house and hide when she arrived home from work?

As she drove through the gate to Caroline and Noah's house, Jo promised to put the intimidation of Chase aside for her working hours. Maybe during Tyler's quiet time, she could investigate the security systems. She would worry about it later.

The usual morning chaos reigned, and Jo waded into the breakfast preparations for the children, helping with the parents' lost items. When both adults left, dispensing kisses to their children and thanking Jo, the only noises were the crunch of cereal and toast as the kids ate.

Today, she had to take the kids to playgroup, and for the first time since starting this job, Jo considered not going. Tyler grumbled when she mentioned the prospect of having a quiet day at home. Would Noah and Caroline likely be angry if she kept the kids home?

"Jo, it's finger painting today! We have to go."

With a silent groan, she conceded that finger painting beat a quiet day at home, hands down.

Once they arrived at the playgroup, she focused on covering children and toddlers in great lengths of plastic and wiping their faces and arms. Jo discovered that finger painting was a misnomer; the paint may start on the fingers, but soon migrates to faces, arms, other children, and clothes. The mums fussed at the mess, but James, late as always, appeared unconcerned with the state of Caroline and Amy's clothes.

"What's the problem?" he asked. "The clothes wash, and if you hose the kids outside, you minimise the mess inside the house." While Jo and James laughed at the absurdity of that statement, other mothers responded with appalled expressions and disgusted looks.

"Lighten up, ladies; it was a joke!" James said.

The playgroup was for children to socialise, but surely the parents should enjoy it too? Jo loathed these get-togethers. Hostile glares and scrutiny were the order of the day, and she felt more unwelcome each time she arrived. After the busy morning, Jo carried Maddy towards the car; the little girl had run out of energy. As Jo placed Maddy in the car seat, her phone buzzed; a message popped up on the screen. Jo tensed, barely able to make herself check the text. Just as she had feared, the message was another threat from Chase.

'I'm watching you, bitch. I will have the money you owe me.'

Jo swung around and scanned the other cars parked near hers. No one looked suspicious. Would Chase use his car or drive a less visible vehicle? As she tried to do Maddy's belt up, her hands shook. Was she putting the children in danger? Thoughts and questions whirled around in her head. She had to leave now, but the roads to Caroline's place were in an unpopulated region. If he ran her off the road or accosted her, there would be no one to help.

Jo cried out in alarm when a hand grasped her shoulder. She swung around to see James looking at her, concern in his eyes.

"Are you okay?"

She nodded her head. "Sure."

James scrutinised her pale face and wild eyes. "You look like you've seen a ghost."

Tears welled in her eyes.

James shook his head. "That's not convincing if I say so myself. Follow me home, and we can talk."

"What about the busybodies? There is talk about us already."

"Jo, you and I know we are friends, and so does Rachel, so stuff the others."

Jo sat in Rachel and James' kitchen with a mug clasped in her hand. The colour had returned to her face, and the tears had dried. She told James all about her shameful marriage and her attempt to end the farce.

"God, Jo! Do you trust this solicitor whose office leaks information to the enemy?"

"I trust Barry, but the information must come from his office. He says my file is locked, so how has Chase found my phone number? He frightens me. What if he arrives here?"

James rubbed her hand over his chin. "Could you get a restraining order or something?"

"Barry said he would see about it, but Chase won't let a minor detail like that get in the way. I must tell Caroline; I don't want to endanger the kids."

"Is he dangerous?"

Jo shook her head. "I'm not positive, but he has made threats to Barry. He sent aggressive messages so that he might be dangerous."

Chapter Twenty-One

Jo kept her eye on the rear-view mirror as she drove toward Caroline and Noah's place. No traffic was on the road, and she was undecided whether this was a good thing. The stop at James' house had put her behind schedule, and Maddy had fallen asleep in the car seat.

Jo surveyed the surroundings, looking for anything unusual as she carried Maddy into the house. She placed the toddler into her cot and returned to the kitchen to feed Tyler. To her surprise, Noah sat at the table, talking to the little boy. When Tyler saw Jo, he looked at his father. Noah nodded, and Tyler grabbed a banana and left the room.

"Sit down!" growled Noah.

Jo's eyes widened, and she tilted her head to one side. What the hell was this? Without comment, she sat. She watched Noah; he glared at her.

"Where did you go after playgroup?"

"You could have asked without shouting at me. We went to James' place because..."

Noah stood up and towered over Jo. "I will not have my children dragged around the countryside while you conduct affairs with other men. Rachel may not care what you're doing with her husband, but I will not have my kids put at risk."

"Wait, Noah, I..."

"Get your things and get out. You're fired! Never come near my children again. We trusted you."

"Please, Noah, it's not what you think."

"Don't speak. If you're still here in two minutes, I'll call the police. Get out of my house!"

Jo stumbled away from the house, tears streaming down her face. Noah glared at her from the front veranda with a look of total disgust. The drive into town felt like it lasted forever, and Jo was numb as she navigated the bends and curves of the dirt road. What had happened that had sent Noah into such a rage? Jo spoke to Caroline, and they sorted out this friendship thing. Why was Noah so angry? The familiar view of the lovely old Queenslander she called home saddened her. Did she have to move? She couldn't stay in a town where one of its most prominent citizens believed she was a slut. She felt bone-tired as she pulled herself out of the car.

What did she do to make the world hate her so much? She changed her life, lost half her body weight, and became healthier and fitter, yet none of that mattered to the world. Jo wanted to gorge herself on rubbish food for the first time since her life-changing experience at the retreat. The problem with the urge to comfort eat was that she had nothing in the house that tempted her.

Noah watched Jo leave, anger and disappointment crushing him. When Jo started as their nanny, he was grateful not only that the kids loved her but also that she made Caroline's life easier. In the evening, before they found Jo, Caroline had to cook tea, bring in the washing, and do a million other chores that Jo now did before Caroline returned from the shop. He had called in randomly and always found the kids engaged and happy; why did she have to coerce another woman's husband?

Jo's affair with James was bound to come out in a community as small as Mountain View. Gossip was the currency in a small town; everybody knew everyone else's business, so how had Jo thought to keep her liaisons with James a secret? Did she believe that using his kids as camouflage would work, that nobody would question how often she met James if they had their kids with them?

Noah dreaded informing Caroline because, without Jo, they were back to square one regarding childcare. Even though he tried to pick up family duties where he could, dragging two little kids around the farm while he was planting or harvesting crops wasn't practical. Damn, Jo, had done a police check, but there were so many sins that weren't illegal, even if they weren't moral.

After learning about his personal history, he wondered how Mark would handle a cheating tenant. Would he evict Jo or leave her renting his house, even though she was breaking up a family? Surely Rachel couldn't condone James and Jo's relationship, and Noah wondered if she had first known about the affair when the busybodies told her. Did she have suspicions, or was she blindsided like he was?

Damn, why did the woman seem to be the answer to their prayers but was a home-wrecking hussy?

Chapter Twenty-Two

As Marc pulled into his favourite spot outside the café, he remembered the first day he met Jo. He'd been incredibly rude to her, yet she'd forgiven him and put the incident behind her. His worry about becoming too attached to any woman, particularly her, had made him push her away. He ran his tongue over his lips, trying to recall the taste and feel of her. God, he had it bad. Maybe she'd be willing to have a fling, which might get her out of his system.

Once Marc pulled the café door open, welcoming aromas met him. He hadn't realised how hungry he was, but his stomach rumbled, reminding him he hadn't eaten morning tea. Lindsay greeted Marc, and he had just taken his seat when a gaggle of women entered the room. Chatting seriously and with expressions ranging from thrilled to disgusted, the women discussed a scandal of enormous proportions. Marc wasn't interested in their discussion until he heard Jo's name. He turned to look at the women, who were happy to include him in their conversation.

"Marc, how can you have that shameless hussy living in your house? The affair between Jo and James devastated Rachel; this will probably end their marriage," said Natalie Frost. "Alice and I have seen them cavorting in front of those little children at the park."

Alice agreed. "We can see them every Thursday in the park. They don't care who knows. It's disgraceful!"

Marc looked enquiringly at Lindsay. She shrugged her shoulders and raised her eyebrows.

"Is there anything more to it than just sitting in the park in broad daylight?" Marc asked.

"Yes! Sonia says they are as thick as thieves in the playgroup. They sit together and converse. They rarely talk to the other mothers or join in any conversations."

Lindsay butted in. "That's hardly a crime. If I went to a playgroup, I wouldn't want to talk about breastfeeding or potty training. Jo is a nanny, not a mum, and James is a bloke. What interest would either of them have in the conversation if the others always talk about babies?"

"That might be so, but Jo and James went to his house after playgroup. Sonia lives just down the road from James and Rachel, and she said that Jo was there for more than an hour," volunteered Natalie.

Marc didn't want to believe that Jo and James were having an affair, but the evidence seemed pretty damning.

"What has Rachel got to say about these allegations?"

"She denied any wrongdoing on her husband's part. She laughed it off when I told her what was happening, but I could tell she was upset." Alice said.

The conversation killed Marc's appetite; he would have walked away with nothing if he hadn't already ordered. As he ploughed through his meal, Marc found it hard to reconcile the woman he knew with this femme fatale about whom the women were talking. If this information was correct, did he have any obligation to the community to remove her from the district? His grandparents' house had been empty for years, and Jo loved the place. Although he hadn't been inside since she moved in, Lindsay said Jo had spent a fortune furnishing the house with items consistent with the building's age.

Having zoned the conversation out, Marc was stunned when he heard Alice say, "You know, of course, that she's running away from her husband?"

"Where did you hear that?" Lindsay demanded.

Alice gave a cat-like smile and said, "Oh, I have my sources. She is supposed to have cheated on him and taken off with lots of his money."

"I know Jo better than you ladies do, and I'm telling you that whoever gave you the information is lying to you," Lindsay said.

"Oh, no, I got this from the horse's mouth."

Marc felt sick. He knew what it was like to be the victim of a lying, cheating woman. Sympathy for Jo's wronged husband welled up. He balled his fists as he thought of the woman he had loved who had cheated on him with his friend. How did her husband feel? Not only had she cheated on him, but she had taken off with his money. This lady, who loved his house, had stolen money from a wronged spouse to furnish his home. If this were the case, Jo would have to go. She could move all her ill-got gains out of his house and hit the road as far as he was concerned. He couldn't believe he was again attracted to a lying, cheating thief.

An hour later, Marc pulled up outside his grandparents' house. Lindsay had told him that the furnishings in the house were suitable for its age and style, and Jo had also spent her husband's money on authentic-looking planters and veranda furniture. Marc's stomach churned with remembered hurts and deceptions from his best friend and fiancée. No way was he going there again; Jo had to go.

When she opened the door, it was only as far as the safety chain allowed. After recognising Marc, she closed the door, and he heard the chain sliding across. Even as angry as he was, Marc registered that Jo had checked who he was before moving the chain. That was a telltale sign. Was she scared that her husband would turn up and feared the retribution he might claim? The door opened wide, and the first thing Marc saw was the puffy, red eyes that told him she had been crying. Jo tried a weak smile, but the angry look on Marc's face didn't bode well for the conversation she knew was coming.

"What can I do for you?"

"I'm angry that you took me in. All that stuff about never being hit on or told you were hot was all lies. God, I'm stupid! An attractive face, and I'm a believer. Well, the patrons at the cafe have set me straight. We don't want your kind in our community, so you have a week to vacate the property. When your husband comes for you, I don't want my name associated with you. You have a week. That's all. I'll send anything left to welfare at the end of the week."

Marc strode away from the house. As he climbed into his vehicle, he realised Jo had not said a word, although it was probably hard to justify breaking up a family.

Jo watched as Marc drove away. His barbs had pierced her heart. She stood transfixed with shock at the things he had said. Her head felt fuzzy, and her limbs were so heavy that she couldn't move enough to go inside. She collapsed into one of the veranda chairs. After the fiasco that was her marriage, didn't she deserve some kindness in her life? As the tears ran down her face, she wrapped her arms around herself and rocked backwards and forwards in a keening motion.

When night fell, Jo went inside. The house that had given her a sense of belonging and peace was no longer her home. Marc had told her to get out, and Noah had fired her. Her first impression of Mountainview had been spot on, and she should have followed her instincts and left before Marc had convinced her to eat breakfast.

Chapter Twenty-Three

Jo was emotionally and physically exhausted when she pulled into the Happy Wanderer motel car park. Even though she didn't drive at night, she abandoned Mountainview immediately. God only knew who might arrive tomorrow to question her morals. She hoped James hadn't received the same treatment. She was glad that she and James had discussed their association and would always be grateful that Rachel felt secure enough in her relationship with James to allow the friendship to continue.

Once she organised pizza delivery, she searched her laptop for industrial cleaners and removers. Tomorrow, she planned to hire the removers to pack and collect her belongings from Marc's house, and when they finished, the industrial cleaners could clean the house. The house wasn't dirty, but she wanted to ensure he didn't accuse her of trashing the place.

Jo wanted to ring Barry and unload all her woes on him, but, looking at the time of night, she decided that tomorrow was soon enough to brief him. She needed to tell him she was moving on and organise for him to pay for the removalist, storage, and cleaners. Once again, she would head off into the country to find the right place to live.

The morning light shining through the cheap curtains woke her. She lay in bed, trying to get her bearings for a few minutes. When recognition hit, the memory of what happened yesterday rushed back into her mind. Dragging herself out of bed, she threw on her running clothes and left the depressing little room.

After breakfast, she called the removers, who were experiencing a lull in business, and asked them to start the next day. After she rang and organised the cleaners, she needed to call Barry. While she waited for the phone to ring, Jo tapped her fingers on the bench. Barry's receptionist answered.

"Hi, Ange, it's Jo Bromley here. I wondered if Barry was available to take a phone call."

"Can he ring you back? He is meeting with a client at the moment."

"Sure, I'll wait for his call."

Jo updated him on the previous day's events when Barry called back. She found it challenging to repeat the details, and she was weeping when she finished her tale.

"Gee, you've got to be kidding? What small-town mentality conceives of that stuff? What has James said?"

"I haven't spoken to James; it might worsen his situation. He has to live in the town, but I can escape. I'm staying in a motel in Lakeside. I have organised removers and cleaners. When the contractors finish, I'll ring Marc and suggest he inspect the property. After he looks through the house, I'll return the keys and leave."

"Jo, I'm sorry. I thought you had found the right place to live. There are plenty of places in Queensland that you haven't checked out. Let me know when you leave Lakeside so I can check on you. Okay?"

"Yeah, I will."

As she opened the door of the old Queenslander, a wave of sadness swept over her. Her belongings and the furniture were gone, and the house was now spotlessly clean. This lovely old home looked abandoned. She saw the possibilities when she first visited the house, but now all she saw was heartbreak. The last thing she needed to do was hand the keys back to Marc, but she insisted he inspect the property before she left. No way would he accuse her of damaging this lovely old building. The car's sound in the driveway pulled Jo back from her thoughts. She walked out onto the veranda and watched as Marc approached. His tall, lithe body looked relaxed as he strolled towards the house. Her nerves tingled as he got closer, and her pulse raced when he stepped onto the veranda.

"Why do I need to check the house? You should have left the keys at the café and saved me the bother."

Jo shook her head. "You need to inspect it because you have accused me of cheating and stealing, and I don't need you accusing me of trashing your house. Just look at it, and then you can have the keys, and I will be out of your life."

Marc scrutinised her. Her shiny hair swung near her jaw in that cheeky bob, but her face was pale, and her cheeks had a rosy glow of anger or embarrassment. She looked sad, and he didn't understand how someone who cheated and stole from their spouse could be sentimental enough to become attached to this old house. With a shake of his head, Marc strode into the building and walked through the rooms. The place was spotless, with no damage to the paintwork or walls.

"Yeah, that's fine. If you give me the keys, you can leave."

"Marc, you're all making a mistake. I don't understand why.."

"Stop, Jo. Nothing you say will fix what you have done."

Marc strode away from the house. As he eased his vehicle onto the main road, he slammed the brakes as a red sports car tore past him towards the house. Nobody around there drove a sports car, so it must be the wealthy husband. He shrugged; Jo was going to get her retribution.

Jo collapsed onto the veranda stairs just as a car sped along the track to her house. Was Marc coming back? The engine's tone and the vehicle's pace alerted Jo to the imminent danger. As she jumped to her feet, her husband raced up the stairs. She tried to fight him off, but he overpowered her.

"Well, well, wifey dear. Don't you look remarkable? I could almost go for you now you aren't fat and disgusting." Chase flicked her hair with his fingers and ran his eyes over her body.

"We might have fun while we sort out this money thing."

"Don't touch me, you pig. We don't need to sort out anything. Where do you reckon I'm getting the money? I worked here as a nanny to pay my bills."

"We'll sort that out when we get back home. Get in the car; we're leaving."

Chase grabbed Jo's arm and pushed her towards his vehicle. She gripped the door handle of her SUV as Chase pulled her past it, but he broke her hold and bundled her into the passenger side of the car. Jo grasped the door release when he moved around the bonnet to get into the driver's seat and pulled. Nothing happened. Chase laughed at her as he buckled up his seatbelt.

"Childproof locks; who could believe a sports car would have childproof locks?"

Jo slumped in the seat, defeated. Her abduction would raise no interest in town. Chase had to drive right past the café to reach the main road, but she couldn't alert the patrons to her plight. The locals had painted her as a scarlet lady, and no one would raise a hand to help her. She realised that, once again, she was on her own.

Chase sped through town and onto the road that had led her here months ago. The drive home took four days; she had to spend shut up with this bully, her husband.

"You could make this easy on yourself if you paid me. I'll settle for two million dollars."

Jo choked. "Two million dollars. Are you delusional? I inherited a large house from my father and one business, which I later sold. I sold the contents of my house and used the money left over to buy and furnish that lovely old Queenslander." Jo hoped whoever gave Chase directions to the house hadn't spilled the beans that it was a rental.

"I worked for a living as a nanny. If I had lots of money, why would I bother working?"

"Your job was just to put me off the track. It's a ruse. What do you know about being a nanny?"

"I'm excellent at it, and I loved the job. Give it up, Chase. Let me go, and I'll call Barry to give you another thirty thousand dollars. That's all I can offer. I refuse to live in a humpy just so you and that tart of yours can swan around and appear important."

Chase lashed out with his hand and connected with Jo's face. The hit pushed her sideways and smashed her head into the doorjamb. The impact of the double blow made her head swim, and nausea rolled in her stomach. Her stomach heaved.

"I'm going to be sick". Chase shrieked in rage and slowed. He realised he had engaged the childproof locks when he leaned over her and gripped the door handle. He pulled over, and the tyres slid in the thick gravel at the side of the road. Jo shrieked as the car's back end slid out, and the vehicle careened across the road.

Chase lashed out again, this time connecting with her jaw. Jo curled herself into a ball to make herself a smaller target for her enraged husband. When the car stopped, he rushed around the bonnet to open the door. Even though Jo still had her seatbelt on, Chase tried to pull her out of the car. When his efforts were unsuccessful, he screamed at her.

"Undo yourself, bitch. Get your fat arse out of my car."

On hands and knees, Jo levered herself out of the car and onto the side of the road. Her stomach lurched, and she vomited. With her head hanging, she didn't see the next blow until the boot landed in her ribs.

"Get off the ground; we don't have time for you to be fooling."

Jo looked at this man and wondered what had turned him into an animal. Was his natural charm a scam to trick her into the marriage? With tears rolling down her cheeks, Jo tried to pull herself into a sitting position. She was frightened that she might receive another kick if she didn't protect her ribs. As Jo staggered to her feet, she glanced at Chase and waited for what came next. She watched her enraged husband and didn't hear the car stop near them. When the sound of a door closing and footsteps approaching registered in her brain, she looked at the newcomer. It took her a moment or two to realise that the car was a highway patrol vehicle and its occupant was a tall, overweight police officer. She wept with relief.

"Can I help, folks?" he asked.

Jo opened her mouth to speak, and Chase grabbed her arm.

"My wife is sick. She'll be right in a few minutes."

Jo wrenched herself away from Chase and gasped, "Help me, please."

The police officer said, "Okay, mate, let go of the lady, and we can sort this out."

Chase seized her arm, hauling her towards the car. As Chase twisted her arm viciously, she screamed and lashed out with her foot, kicking his leg. With a savage curse, he limped towards his vehicle.

"Stop!" yelled the officer, but Chase gunned the engine and took off. The back of the car fishtailed as Chase tried to put as much distance as possible between himself, the policeman, and his wife. He vowed the bitch would pay for all the trouble she had caused him. While swearing vengeance on his wife, Chase overcorrected the car, and the vehicle headed straight into the path of a large truck. The truck driver blared his horn in warning, and Chase wrenched the wheel to the side. Jo gasped as Chase's car careered through the long grass at the road's edge. The vehicle hurtled over an embankment and ploughed headfirst into a large gum tree.

Shattering glass and shrieking metal filled the air, and then the world seemed to move in slow motion.

Chapter Twenty-Four

Most of the town's citizens were at the coffee shop. When Caroline and Noah entered the café, it was apparent they were at odds. There hadn't been a more enthralling scandal for years.

"What are all these people doing here?" Caroline asked Lindsay. In a quick summary, Lindsay updated Caroline. "I'm concerned for her. She was afraid of her husband and tried to get a restraining order. I'm positive he's got her. What should we do?"

Caroline glanced around the room, her eyes alighting on Marc. When she walked over to him, he held his palms outstretched. "Don't look at me, Caroline. Whatever you're doing, leave me out of it."

"You need to drive out to Jo's and see if it looks like she left in a hurry. We need her mobile phone; if her husband forced her to go, it would still be at the house."

"Why me?"

"Because you own the property and can legally go inside. If I ring Rachel, she and James should be here when you return."

Marc shook his head. "She won't be there; I evicted her. She only returned to the house this morning to give me the key."

Noah stood in front of Caroline. "Mind your own business, Caro. It has nothing to do with you."

Caroline planted her hands on her hips. "I should mind my business like you and all these busybodies here minded their business. Not likely; I intend to rectify the harm that the gossiping busybodies caused, and then I aim to help Jo. Too bad if you disagree."

With a disgusted look, Noah stalked towards the door. "Coming?" he snapped at Marc. Marc threw up his hands in surrender and followed Noah. The drive back to Jo's place was silent, as the men fumed at having to aid a stranger who had put the entire town at odds with each other. Marc broke the silence, shaking his head and saying,

"We should have got the cops to do this. If the husband is there, this might get ugly."

"If it looks like it will turn violent, we'll call the cops. I don't want to get caught up in Jo's mess. Thank God I discovered what she was doing before she jeopardised the kids."

Marc and Noah drove into the driveway. The door to her SUV stood open, and her phone was on the console. When they investigated further, they discovered that the house doors were unlocked and the lights were on. Even to the most sceptical person, Jo had not left the scene voluntarily.

"What does Caro know we don't?" Noah asked Marc.

"I do not know, but she's your woman. Why didn't you discuss this?"

Noah shook his head, and after turning off the lights and securing the property, he and Marc headed back to Lindsay's place armed with the mobile.

As Marc and Noah parked the car, Rachel, James, and the two kids headed toward the cafe's front door.

"This could be awkward. I'll stay out here," Marc said.

"Not on your life, mate. If I have to go inside, you do too."

The bell on the door rang, and the noise in the room subsided. Noah said, "You were right. She didn't go willingly. She didn't lock up, the lights were on, and she left this," he said, holding up the phone.

Natalie spoke, voicing her point of view to the room. "Why do we care? She's getting what she deserves if her husband has seized her. He said she cheated on him and stole his money, and now she's involved with James."

Lindsay glared at the woman. "You have interfered in people's lives without learning the truth. Why did you tell her husband where she was before checking that it was okay? I know why; you're a busybody with no life of your own."

Caroline tapped on the side of the glass, calling for silence.

"There are things we need to do. First, we need to report that Jo's husband has kidnapped her and later, we'll work out the issues that have emerged here."

Caroline put out her hand, and Marc gave her the phone. There were a few numbers on speed dial, and Caroline resolved to try the first number and work through them if needed. Caroline knew Jo had a sister, so she guessed that the first number might be hers, but she didn't want to alarm the sister, so she tried the second number. The second number she tried was Barry's, and once Caroline told him of her fears, the case moved quickly. Barry had the car's make, model, and registration and reported Jo's kidnapping to the police.

When Barry rang back a few minutes later, he said, "The police have started a watch for the car, so when we have something to report, I'll call you," Barry promised.

Caroline relayed Barry's conversation with those in the room. She turned to face James and Rachel.

"Now, for our problems here. Rachel and James come over here. Everyone needs to hear what you have to say."

Rachel took the lead. She turned to face the gossipers and said, "My husband, James, is not having an affair with Jo. Please do not give me those pitying looks. James and Jo are friends. If you have friends, you spend time with them. We all had this discussion a long time ago."

"And," Caroline said, "If you choose not to trust the couple concerned, trust me. Jo and I had that conversation a while ago. It never worried me that my children were in any moral danger, and I was glad Jo had made a friend she trusted."

James stood. "Thanks, Rach and Caroline. Jo and I became friends because neither of us is interested in discussing breastfeeding or potty training at the playgroup. Without her to have an adult conversation, I would have quit going a long time ago. She spent an hour at my place the other day because she received a threatening text message from her husband and needed someone to confide in. She agreed I could tell

Rach, but she was sure that neither of us would spread her problems around the town. I won't break her confidence except to say that her husband cheated on her on their honeymoon and married her for the fortune he thinks she has. When he continued to spend most nights with his girlfriend, only coming home in the morning to shower and change for work, Jo filed for divorce. Anything else you think you know is wrong. Those are the facts."

The café's inhabitants weighed the information James had shared with them. The noise in the room increased as people discussed the case.

While they waited for news, Lindsay served meals to the townsfolk, who had developed an appetite; time dragged on, despite the food being a distraction. The animated conversations that had followed James' disclosure grew less vigorous as the seriousness of the situation sank in. As the time ticked away, Carolyn and Lindsay began to panic. How long could it take the police to find such a distinctive vehicle? What if the police failed to find Jo before her husband hurt her? A ringing sound halted the noise, and Caroline answered Jo's phone.

"This is Caroline."

"Caroline, it's Barry. The police picked Jo up a hundred kilometres from Mountainview. The highway patrolman stopped to see if they needed help because the car was on the side of the road. Chase had a car accident, and he died at the scene. The rescue helicopter picked Jo up on the road there, and she was on her way to the city hospital. Her injuries are not life-threatening."

Tears welled in Caroline's eyes, and her fingers shook.

"Was Jo in the car accident with Chase?"

"No," Barry said. "The bastard assaulted her. She has head and facial injuries and broken ribs. I'll give you another update after I've seen her. Okay?"

"Yes, sure. Thanks, Barry."

The mood in the café turned sombre as people digested the news of Jo's condition. The gossipers had hurried from the building, and those remaining discussed how to help Jo.

"Why didn't you tell me you had that conversation with Jo?" Noah asked Caroline.

"God, I feel terrible. It was the day you went to the chamber of commerce meeting and got home so late that I was asleep. After that, it slipped my mind. You never listen to gossip, so I didn't think it was important."

Noah shook his head. "Because of our lack of communication, I fired the best thing that has happened to us in a long time. The kids miss Jo, and I've made life harder for you. How do we fix this?"

"I don't know if we can," Caroline said.

Chapter Twenty-Five

Jo lay in bed, the hum of people walking along the corridor comforting in this sterile room. The doctor she had seen the previous day said she could go home later that day. The broken ribs, cuts and bruises were not enough to keep her hospitalised, but yesterday's events had left her with a concussion, so they admitted her for observation overnight.

Footsteps outside the door warned her of Barry's arrival. Watching as he walked towards her, a wave of guilt washed over her. Barry, who usually dressed well and remained in control, looked bedraggled and stressed. If she hadn't left the disaster of her life for Barry to sort out, he wouldn't be here now.

"Hi, Jo. How are you this morning?"

"I'm fine. I want to get out of here and go home. The problem is that I don't have a home anymore."

"Sorry, even if you decide where home is, we still need to talk to the police and organise Chase's funeral. I guess he left a will; we might try to contact his girlfriend for that."

A man in a white coat arrived and interrupted the conversation. "How are you today, Mrs Donaldson?"

"I'm fine and ready to leave if you think I'm right to go."

"I'll need to check the strapping on the ribs and the other cuts and contusions." The doctor looked over at Barry. "Might we have privacy?"

Barry jumped from his chair. "I'll settle the bill, and if the doctor is satisfied, we'll be ready to go."

The doctor released Jo from the hospital, and Barry drove them to the police station. They both filled out statements, and Jo informed the officer of Chase's escalating, irrational behaviour and threats.

The officer looked up from the paperwork laid out on the desk. "At the moment, the threats are unsubstantiated, and while it changes, nothing, a copy of the text messages, might help determine his state of mind. Can you access those messages?"

"It might take a little while. I couldn't grab my phone before Chase abducted me, so it was still in Mountain View. Can you wait a minute, and I'll see if someone can email those texts?"

The police officer nodded. Now Jo had a problem to tackle.

Jo knew Caroline had her phone, but she doubted Caroline would answer it even if it were nearby. Jo called after an internet search for Lindsay's business phone number.

"Hello, this is Lindsay's Eatery."

"Lindsay, it's Jo Bromley."

"Jo, how are you? When are you coming home?" Jo's eyes welled with tears. The mention of Mountainview as her home was a balm to her aching heart. She cleared her throat. "Not sure yet, but I need help. Caroline called Barry on my phone when Chase kidnapped me, and I need stuff from the phone. Does Caroline still have it?"

"Yeah, she does, and without a nanny, she has had to curtail her business. She should be home; do you want her number?"

"Yes, please, that's why I rang you. The number is on my phone, but I don't remember it as I always press speed dial."

After a brief conversation with Caroline, the messages arrived on the police officer's computer. The officer scrolled through Chance's posts.

"Okay, definitely escalating. Was your husband always irrational, Mrs Donaldson?"

Jo shook her head. "When we met, he was charming, but after the wedding, he changed. Office workers in my business speculated that he married me for my money. After I filed for divorce, his demands for money became increasingly outrageous and culminated in my kidnapping. He lost the plot somewhere along the line."

"Okay, I'm satisfied with your explanations. You can leave as long as you leave your contact details. I can't imagine that there will be any more questions. It all appears straightforward."

A thought struck Jo, and she queried Barry.

"Did you find out where the leak at your firm was?

"Yeah, and let me say how sorry I am. I employed a temp to fill in for Marcie, who was on long service leave. It turns out that the fill-in secretary was best friends with Chase's girlfriend. Initially, she accessed my office, and after I removed your details, she hacked my home computer. I placed you in danger and will always feel guilty for that. The outcome could have been worse except for the helpful highway patrolman."

Once Barry organised a transport truck to collect his car, he and Jo flew home. Barry hired a car at the airport, and Jo caught a taxi to Hope's house.

"God, I can't believe he turned into such a loonie. When we set our plan into action, I thought he would settle for a payout."

"He wanted a payout, but I wasn't paying him the two million dollars he wanted."

Hope gasped. "Two million dollars, you're kidding me!"

"I'm not kidding, and now I have to pay for a funeral for the blighter."

After spending the next day looking at funerals, Jo threw her hands in the air. "I never met his friends or family; I do not know what kind of funeral he wanted. Why do I get to do this?"

Hope looked at Jo for a minute. "I've got an idea. The police gave you his effects back, didn't they?"

"Yes, but what good will they be? Most of the stuff I bought."

Hope grinned. "I said I've got an idea. Where is his phone?"

Jo rummaged around in the cabinet's drawer where she had placed Chase's belongings. When she held up the phone, Hope said, "Do you want out of planning the funeral?"

"Hell, yes."

"Okay, big sister, look and learn." Hope powered up the phone and scrolled through the contacts. Kellie's number was on speed dial, so Hope pressed the number and waited for a response.

"Jo, you slag, how could you use Chase's phone to ring me?" screamed the voice of Chase's girlfriend.

"This isn't Jo; it's Hope. I'm Jo's sister, and I want to make you an offer. Instead of screaming, listen."

"What's the offer?" snapped Kelly

"Well, we know Chase married Jo for her money and that he continued to see you even after they married. As you were the person closest to him, Jo and I decided you might prefer to organise the funeral instead of us."

"She cheated him out of the money he should have gotten for marrying her. Now, you want to land me with the bill for his burial?"

"If you stop being belligerent, I will tell you how this will work. Jo will pay for the funeral, but you can organise the service. Jo has never met his friends or extended family, so asking you to arrange the service seems reasonable. If you don't want to do it, we will hold a private service, and none of his mates, relatives, or you will be there. The decision is yours."

After a moment's silence, Kellie said, "I don't know how to arrange a funeral."

"That's easy," said Hope. "Look up a funeral director in the phone book or online, and they will walk you through it after you meet with them. The invoices must go to Jo's solicitor, and Barry will pay the expenses. Please do us a favour and don't run the bill up to an enormous amount to spite Jo. You need to take responsibility for what happened, and Jo was the innocent victim of your scam."

Kelly grunted. "Does Jo want to go to the funeral?"

"No, she doesn't. Oh, and Chase's belongings that the police returned are here: his wallet, the phone, and a bag of things he had with him. We will return those to you if you tell me where to send them."

Once Jo and Hope dealt with the problem of Chase's funeral, Jo stayed and visited with her sister for a while. Her bruising had faded but was yet to disappear, and her ribs still hurt. She wasn't up to dealing with the problems she left behind in Mountainview.

Chapter Twenty-Six

Jo gazed out the window as Barry drove through the countryside. There had been flowers and well-wishes from the townsfolk, but the knowledge that the town residents believed she was a woman with loose morals made returning a task she would have happily missed. Six weeks after her abduction, Jo wasn't positive if any of her life in Mountainview remained.

As the car crested the rise, Barry let out a whistle.

"Now I understand why you liked this place. It looks magical, huddled into the mountain, the water cutting it in half."

When Jo remained silent, Barry raised an eyebrow.

"I guess you're concerned with this reunion."

Jo looked through the windscreen, but she had turned her focus inward and didn't see the breathtaking scenery.

"Everyone in the town branded me a slut. Only Lindsay, Caroline, James and Rachel thought otherwise. How do I face these people? What do I say to people when I meet them on the street?"

"Jo, if there's one thing I've learned about you in the last month, it's that you're strong. Yes, you've faced hard times, but you've recovered. Treat people with understanding and a smile. Nothing makes people more uneasy than when you're courteous, and they know they deserve harsh words."

Jo's stomach clenched, and her pulse raced as the vehicle glided through the familiar streets. It was okay for Barry to give advice, but she was the one who had to face the malicious gossipers of the town.

"Where do you want to go first?" Barry's question pulled Jo out of her preoccupation with the forthcoming meetings.

"Go to the café. Most people will be there, and I need the keys to get into the house. I hope they replaced my furniture."

Barry pulled into the spot Marc had said was his place when she first arrived. Jo gave a wry grin. She wondered if Marc would challenge

Barry for the position. Jo exited the car after taking a deep breath to fortify herself. Barry placed his hand on the small of her back, and they walked to the café's doorway.

When the doorbell announced their entry, the few patrons who sat eating or drinking focused on the two newcomers. Lindsay looked up, and a smile blossomed on her face. She came around the counter and gave Jo a bear hug.

"Welcome back to Mountainview. You've had two shots at living here, but they say the third time is the charm. Please give us one more chance at getting this right."

"Thanks. Lindsay, please meet my friend and solicitor, Barry. Aside from you, will it please anyone else I've returned?"

"Hi, Barry. Yes, people will be glad to see you, but there's discomfort in the neighbourhood. Criticising someone is easy, but it's much harder to apologise for malicious slights. Just give it time. I know Noah is falling over himself to apologise to you. Noah and Caroline's communication broke down, so he believed the gossipers who targeted him."

"Are my keys here, or must I find Marc?"

"I have the keys here. Will you come back for dinner and meet the others?"

"I guess I might as well get it over with."

When they left the café, Jo wondered if she was brave enough to return tonight. The only thing that convinced her to meet the people who had started the gossip and those who perpetuated it was that if she didn't show up today, she would have endless awkward visits from the townsfolk. As the house came into view, Jo smiled. "I've always loved this house. It felt like home as soon as I saw it."

"It suits you better than that monstrosity you had in town."

"Yeah, I'm a different person living here. I loved living here before Chase found me, and the gossipers upped the ante with malicious rumours. Despite the fuss, I hope I can make this work. Can I turn back time and pretend that none of it happened?"

"No, but you can enjoy reconnecting with your supporters and meeting your detractors head-on. A few ashamed people must want to beg your forgiveness, so the rest is up to you."

Jo entered the house, expecting to see dust covering most surfaces, but the place was spotless, and someone had stocked the fridge with fresh produce.

"Someone has cleaned."

"Marc may have cleaned and been shopping, or one of your new friends may have. I told Marc of your arrival, so it's conceivable he had the house prepared."

Jo walked through the house, reacquainting herself with the lovely old building. She had enjoyed living here, and if all went well, she might ask Mark if he would sell the house, but she didn't want to rush into anything too soon. Her visit to the café tonight would give her an idea of how accepting the community would be.

Jo was apprehensive as Barry again pulled into a park outside the café later that night. The moment of truth was at hand. If people snubbed her or walked out when she arrived, she intended to leave. Lindsay had said the third time was the charm, so the only thing to do was put it to the test. The volume of noise in the room rose. Conversation stopped as the bell jingled over the door, and all eyes focused on the newcomers. Customers all spoke at once, and it overwhelmed Jo when they hugged and kissed her on the cheek. Everyone wanted to make amends for the trouble, and Jo smiled with relief.

Seated at a table, her drink in her hand, a sense of peace enveloped Jo. When Caroline and Noah walked in, Jo stood to hug Caroline. Noah walked towards Jo just as there was a childish shout. "Maddy, look! It's Jo!" Little arms wrapped around her knees as Tyler hugged Jo for all he was worth. Jo leant over and picked up Maddy. The little girl proceeded to choke Jo with the strength of her hug. Noah watched his children and then bowed his head. Caroline noticed her husband's posture and asked Tyler, "Why don't you tell Lindsay what you want, and then you can come back and sit with Jo?"

When Tyler walked away, Noah looked at Jo. As their eyes met, he was furious that he had accepted the lies that the old gossipers had spread.

"Jo, I am so sorry that I believed those women's stories were legitimate. If I hadn't rushed in to protect my children, all the grief and anger might not have happened. My kids miss you and Caroline, and I miss having you both as friends and helpers. Can you forgive me?"

Jo's eyes were shiny with unshed tears. She smiled at Noah and said, "Thank you for your apology. I missed you and the kids. Maybe we can sort out a way for me to visit with the kids."

The shop door opened, and Rachel, James and the girls entered the cafe. James said, "Hey, I heard there was a celebrity here tonight. Welcome home, Jo. We all missed you." The bear hug he gave her was spontaneous and welcoming. Rachel laughed and shook her head.

"Way to go, James. Now, there will be another scandal. We're glad you're back, Jo. We've missed you," she said, hugging Jo.

People came and went throughout the evening, but Jo noticed Marc wasn't there. Each time the bell rang, she looked up to see who was entering, and each time, it disappointed her; it wasn't Marc. Jo called it quits, fatigue making her dizzy. Barry escorted her to the car and slid into the driver's seat.

"That wasn't as awful as you expected. The only person I didn't notice was your landlord. I wonder where he was?"

"He's a solitary person. He couldn't cope with the emotion and happiness of tonight. I'll call him tomorrow to discuss our agreement about eating at the café. For now, all I want to do is crawl into bed."

Jo lay in bed, the sounds of the bush no longer unsettling her now that Chase was no longer a threat. It felt good to reconnect with her friends, but many from the community were absent. Caroline was adamant that the people who were missing were too ashamed to show their faces because the rumours they had started and the information they had given Chase had fatal consequences. That explained some absences, but she still expected to see Mark at the café, despite what Jo had told Barry, even if he said hello and then left. Would she and Mark continue to avoid each other, or might they reach an understanding where they didn't actively dodge each other?

After all that transpired in her relationship with Chase, Jo wasn't in a hurry to find a new man. Having learned from her last relationship, Jo understood that Mark was reluctant to get involved with her, but he kissed her, not the other way around. Jo knew she would drive herself mad if she spent too much time trying to understand Mark's behaviour. With a sigh, she rolled over and put her thoughts on hold. The bush sounds lulled her to sleep at last.

The sun was streaming through the bedroom windows when Jo awoke. She stretched after her best night's sleep in a long time. Pulling on her running gear, Jo headed into the kitchen to grab a drink before her run.

To her amazement, it wasn't Barry sitting at the table with a cup of coffee in front of him; it was Marc.

An "Oh!" of surprise escaped Jo's mouth before she regained her composure.

"To what do I owe the pleasure of your company at this early hour?"

Marc snorted. "Did you look at the clock?"

Jo looked over her shoulder at the clock on the wall above the stove. "Okay, so to what do I owe the pleasure of your company at this late hour?"

"Why don't you grab a coffee, and we can talk?"

Jo's mind swirled with the topics Marc might want to discuss. He appeared to be over his snit, so hopefully, the conversation would be amicable.

"Where's Barry?"

"He said you had nothing worth eating for breakfast and drove to the café just after I arrived."

Mark looked shame-faced.

" God, I don't know where to start. I'm sorry for yelling at you and accusing you of horrid things. After a bad experience with my fiancé and my best friend, I vowed never to trust a girl again. The hurt and anger have consumed my life for the last three years. You shook my world when you came along, and I didn't want it disturbed."

Jo laid her hand on Marc's arm. "Lindsay told me what happened with your fiancé. When I met you, I had no interest in a relationship, no matter how casual it might be. When you are a fat girl, men hit on you when their mates dare them to ask you on a date. They sit at the table, look over their shoulders, and snicker at how fat you are. When Chase chatted me up on a night out and asked for my number, I thought he would never contact me, that he had completed the dare his mates had made. He kept asking me out; he was charming and funny, and I fell for him. There were red flags, but since I had never dated before, I wasn't sure whether I was seeing problems and being overly sensitive. I felt too embarrassed to ask my sister, but I was overjoyed when Chase asked me to marry him. It all fell apart after the ceremony. He cheated while we were on our honeymoon, for God's sake. I quickly discovered that he saw me as a cash cow and was happy as long as I paid his bills. He vowed to make me pay when I filed for divorce, sold the house and cut off his credit card. I thought he did well out of the deal; I paid off his sports car and left him ten thousand dollars in the joint account, but he wanted more. His last demand was for two million dollars."

Mark listened until Jo finished and shook his head.

"Are you telling me you were fat?"

"Yeah, I was. I was a comfort eater, so the more upset I got, the more I ate. When I left town, I decided to drive and see where I ended up. On the way, I came across a health farm, and the proprietor helped me change my eating habits and set up a fitness programme. I've lost sixty kilos since I began my weight loss programme, and I've broken the habit of eating when I'm unhappy."

"God damn, I don't know what to say. After all that happened, I kissed you three times and ran away every time, which you would take as a rejection. I guess I never thought it through from your side; I was trying to protect myself from more heartache, and instead, I hurt you. I'm sorry."

"My one experience in a relationship cured me for life, but when you kissed me, it was like an electric charge surged through my body. You raced away from me every time it happened, and that last time,

I asked you to keep going so I could see if the second time would be painful, messy and embarrassing." Jo giggled. "When Lindsay called in, I could have screamed."

Marc stood up from the table and removed the mug from Jo's hand. Jo's heart swelled when he turned her to face him, and her pulse raced.

"Jo, I've wanted you since that first kiss. If you don't stop me today, I will love you and show you how it should be. Are you okay with that?"

Jo cupped Marc's cheek and her fingers crossed his chest. "Yes, more than you can imagine."

Also by Robyn C Rye

Farnsworth Sisters
Marrying a Rogue
Rescuing Hannah

The Buckingham Sisters
Lady Maggie's Challenge
Layla's Unwanted Husband

The Evans Family
Sometimes Love is not Enough
Still the One
Moving Forward

Standalone
One More Chance
Lady Jayne's Reputation
Third Time's the Charm
Can't Stop Loving You

The Marriage Scam
An Unlikely Match
Searching For You
The Unexpected Suitor
The Lady and the Duke
Starting Over
An Unforgettable Stranger
The Duke's Revenge
The Temporary Wife
Against The Odds
Betrayed
No Good Turn Goes Unpunished
Lady Eloise's Soldier
Lillian's Forbidden Beau
Remember Me
Always Second Best
When One Door Closes
Coming Home to You
Chasing Shadows
Fool Me Once
Deserting Lady Audrey
My Unlikely Saviour
Lies and Deception
A New Beginning
Julia's Second Chance
The Hidden Enemy
The Maiden's Redemption
Miss Elizabeth's Season

www.ingramcontent.com/pod-product-compliance
Lightning Source LLC
Chambersburg PA
CBHW051838130726
47987CB00002B/595